Let Us All Pray Now to Our Own Strange Gods

John Brantingham

World Parade Books

Let Us All Pray Now to Our Own Strange Gods
John Brantingham

First Edition
ISBN# 978-0-6157655-8-7

Cover Art and Design: Michael Turner

Press Contact::
World Parade Books
5267 Warner Avenue #191
Huntington Beach, CA 92649
worldparadebooks.wordpress.com

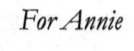

For Annie

Acknowledgements

"Even Puppets Must Die" was published in *Tequila Tales* anthology; "At the Barbershop" was published in *4'33*; "Fish Drop" was published in *Blotter Magazine;* "Harrison Dreams of Murder" was published in *Beatlick News*; "The Sister" was published in *Frogmore Press*. "Harrison's Truck Won't Start" was published in *The Interpreter's House*; "The Monkey Trials" was published in *Verdad*; and "Bees as Metaphor" was published under the title "Bees" in *Booth*; "Giving Carol Away" was published in *Rind Literary Magazine*; "The Phone Call" was published in *The Snailmail Review*; "The Christmas Cabin" was published in *Nite-Writers International Literary Arts Journal;* "Deena's Cabin" was published in *Monomyth*; "Let Us All Pray Now to Our Own Strange Gods" was published in *Confrontation*.

Table of Contents

The Monkey Trials

Harrison doesn't understand what he's seeing at first. He's trying to drive his car into the garage, but it's blocked by some kind of mess strewn across the floor, so he parks in the alley and walks inside, flipping on the extra light as he comes in.

It turns out that it's not a mess, and, in fact, it's pretty well organized. Stanley has arranged most of his stuffed animals in a semicircle facing the back wall, and there seems to be a logic to the seating as well. The monkeys sit up front, ten of them in all, followed by the rabbits and bears in the middle, and the various animals -- porcupines, raccoons, pandas, in the back. He doesn't see what they're facing at first because he's been inspecting the animals on the floor, but Stanley's biggest animal, the orangutan that he calls Big Harry Monk, has been affixed to the wall above the animals.

Harrison bought Big Harry Monk on a business trip five years ago in a little shop specializing in Bigfoot research in Northern California because it was the oddest stuffed animal he'd ever seen. It's about five feet tall, and it's not rigid. The result is an orange stuffed animal with the physique of an out of shape old man, and Harrison has come into Stanley's room again and again to find Big Harry Monk's arms wrapped around his son.

Now it's up on the wall, and Harrison realizes that the stuffed animal has been crucified, one nail through each hand and one through both of his feet. It hangs limply there, and a sign on white computer paper and in purple marker ink has been hung around his drooping head. It says, "Heresy will not be tolerated."

Harrison considers picking up the toys and putting them away, but he doesn't. His car will be fine for one night in the alley, so instead of cleaning, he hits the garage door remote, turns off the light, and goes into the backyard.

Stanley's there, sitting cross-legged under the basketball hoop with two trucks that ram into each other in slow motion. "Zeeear chrsh!" he says as they make contact.

"Hey, Stan," Harrison says.

Stanley's head snaps up and his breath catches in joy. A smile spreads across his face, and he bounces out of his sitting position and into Harrison's arms. "Dad," he says breathlessly. "I thought you were coming home tomorrow."

"No," he says, petting his son's head. "Today." He picks his son up in his arms and the boy clings to his father, legs around Harrison's waist, arms around his neck. "How are you doing, Buddy?"

"I'm great, Dad. I'm on the soccer team." Stanley snuggles his head into Harrison's neck.

"That's great, Stan." He hesitates for a moment. "And I see you've been playing with your animals."

Stanley turns quiet. He looks at Harrison without saying anything, and Harrison has the feeling that he's supposed to drop the subject, and he thinks that might be the best, but he can't seem to make himself do it. Instead, he walks back into the garage, carrying his son. He flips on the light again, and they review the scene. Harrison can feel his son getting warmer in his arms. He's going to ask a question, but Stanley speaks before he can: "I didn't want to do it."

"You didn't want to do what?"

"Mr. Sniggles said that we have to follow the law. He said that there can't be exce . . . excep . . ."

"Exceptions?"

Stanley nods a yes.

"Did you nail him up there all by yourself?"

Stanley nods again.

"What did Big Harry Monk do?"

A tear starts to run down Stanley's cheek, "Heresy," he says. Now that the first drop has come, the boy starts to weep. Tears and snot begin to stream down his face, and he's sobbing in big weeping gasps.

Harrison walks his son out of the garage, petting the boy's hair, and saying, "Hey, hey, it's going to be all right. It's all right, Stan." In a minute or two, he's able to make funny faces until the boy forgets his tears and is chuckling a little. Then he's got the boy laughing out loud, and when he makes a fart noise, Stanley's head falls back, and he screams with the joy only people his age can have.

Harrison puts Stanley down. "Is Mommy inside?" he asks.

"Yes," Stanley says.

"Could you go inside and tell her that I'm home, and I want to talk to her."

Stanley stares at Harrison a moment, working out in his head what Harrison wants. When he figures it out, he nods and runs inside. Harrison watches his son's flatfooted gait and thinks about how much Stan had wanted to be on the soccer team. That's the only thing he allows himself to think about for the time being. The kid really wanted to play soccer, and Harrison's glad that he was able to.

Carol comes out in a minute wiping her hands on her blue jeans. "Harrison?" she asks. "Why don't you come inside?"

"I need to show you something in the garage."

She tilts her head at him. "I'm busy."

He stares at her until she looks at an invisible friend standing to her left and bites her lip. She and her invisible friend exchange glances that say that Harrison's being unreasonable again, that Harrison is pushing and pushing and pushing, and it isn't fair that she's the one who always, always, always has to deal with his moods. Still, though, she follows Harrison into the garage, and when she sees the punishment that has been meted out as a result of the monkey trials, she says, "Oh my God."

"That was my reaction," Harrison says.

"What is this?"

"Haven't you been in here?"

"I've been parking out front." It's true. She's been doing it for a month, and this has become Harrison's space exclusively.

"When do you think he did it?"

Carol turns to the invisible friend standing to her left and narrows her eyebrows in thought. "I don't know," she says.

"Well," Harrison says. His voice cracks. "What night did Joey stay over?"

Harrison can see that she's about to deny it. She and her invisible friend to the left exchange outraged looks, but something inside her deflates, and she just shakes her head. "Thursday," she finally says.

"And he talked about the importance of the law with Stanley, didn't he?"

She nods.

"This has probably been up since Friday then." Harrison tries to work up some anger about it, but he can't yet. Maybe he'll be angry later. Maybe, the moment is so painful to him that he hasn't been able to process his emotions yet, and in an hour or a day, they'll wash over him, and he'll yell and bluster, but the thing is that he doubts it.

"What should we do about it?"

"Counseling?"

"Do you think there's any point?"

"I meant for the boy."

"Ah," Carol says. "Yeah, that makes sense."

Harrison takes a hammer from the tool bench and begins to pull nails out of Big Harry Monk. He can feel Carol watching him. "Why don't you pick up the audience?" he asks. He nods to the semicircle of stuffed animals, and the two of them begin to clean up the monkey trials, careful to keep Stanley's segregation intact. They keep the monkeys with the monkeys in one box, the rabbits and bears in another box, and the other animals in a third box. Big Harry Monk gets a box all of his own.

The Assistant District Attorney

After he's been living in his office for a week, Harrison sees Joey coming out of his front door. His wife's front door, that is. Harrison arrived early to pick his son up for dinner, and he's been sitting here for about ten minutes staring at Joey's Audi thinking to himself that assistant district attorneys aren't paid much, not the way they should be, and Joey has child support payments. He couldn't possibly afford an Audi. That is, he couldn't possibly afford one unless he's taking bribes. He concocts whole scenarios in his mind where Joey is taking bribes from child molesters and drug dealers who smell bad and husbands who beat their wives and mothers who neglect their children. They're the type of people Joey would take bribes from.

Harrison inspects Joey's suit from his seat as Joey gets into the car. He has no eye for fashion, and he's a hundred feet away, but the suit looks expensive. Assistant district attorneys can't afford Audis or expensive suits, not if they're honest, and this man is spending time with his son, hell, maybe he's already moved in, so when Joey pulls away from the curb, Harrison finds himself putting his Ford Ranger into gear and pulling away too, keeping back from the Audi, making sure to drive casually.

Joey turns at the light and drives into the downtown of the little suburb where he lives and where Harrison used to live, but instead of turning left where he would turn if he were going to the courthouse and his office, he turns right. He drives down the side street until he comes to a strip mall and parks in front of a video store specializing in adult movies. Harrison drives by him looking and not looking at him at the same time, and he parks five spaces down in front of a dry cleaners.

By the time he's parked and turned around, Joey's disappeared, presumably into the video store. He aims his cell phone's camera at the store's front door and waits. Joey's so great? Joey's so noble? Harrison never went into a place like this, not the whole time that he knew his wife,

11

and here's Joey doing it within a week of moving into the same house as his son. Harrison dreams of showing the cell phone picture to Carol and that look on her face when she realizes just exactly what it was that she gave up to live with a pervert. That's her word for people into pornography, perverts. She caught Harrison peeking once, and that was the word she used for him. Fine then, she'll see who's the pervert and what she's done to her life, not to mention the boy's.

And just as Harrison's gotten to the point in his fantasy where a weeping Carol begs him to give her another chance and that she didn't know what she was doing, there's a knock at his window that sends Harrison jumping. Joey's standing outside of his truck, arms folded, biting his lower lip.

Harrison lets his head drop, but he has the presence of mind to hit the record function of his cell phone before he puts it on the passenger's seat. When Joey knocks again, Harrison rolls down the window. "What are you doing?"

"Well," Harrison says, "I saw you parking in front of the porno shop, and I wanted to make sure that you weren't buying anything."

"Not that it's any of your business, but I parked there and went into the dry cleaners." He holds up a suit wrapped in plastic. To Harrison's untrained eye, the suit looks expensive.

"Wait a second. It is my business. If you're moving into the same house as my son, you can damn well be sure that I'm going to make you my business. Now, I saw you parking in front of a porno shop, and I wanted to make sure that you weren't bringing smut into my house."

Joey runs his tongue over his teeth and looks to the left and then to the right. Is this something he does in the courtroom? Is this what criminals see the moment before he pounces on them? "No," he says. "You followed me here from *Carol's* house. Then you waited to see if you could blackmail me."

In his mind, Harrison can see himself pulling his fist back and putting it in the middle of Joey's face. He can hear the bones crack, and he imagines himself smashing the man's head on the pavement again and again. In the real world, he stares out the front window. "I didn't plan to blackmail you. If you'd gone in there, I was going to get you out of my son's life."

Joey leans into the cab of the truck, getting into Harrison's personal space. "I want you to understand this," he says quietly. "Hear this. Do you know what I can do to you in this town? Do you know what hell an assistant district attorney can bring to you? I can ruin you, you son of a bitch. You leave me alone, do you hear me?"

Harrison keeps his eyes facing forward. He doesn't say a word.

"I can destroy your life. I can have you arrested. I could charge you with stalking already and conspiracy to blackmail. I'm not talking about making things up. All I have to do is tell the truth."

It doesn't sound right to Harrison. It sounds as though the man is making things up, but he's smart enough to keep his mouth closed.

"This is the last time you and I are going to talk about this."

Joey pulls back and stares at Harrison for another awkward moment. He gets in his too expensive Audi and drives away. He takes the time at the corner stop sign to signal and stop for three second before turning.

When he's out of sight, Harrison sits back in his seat and exhales. His hands are shaking when he reaches for the cell phone, but not so much that he can't see that he recorded the whole conversation. When he plays it back and hears that he got it all, every threat and every syllable, he smiles and pulls out of the space.

He's driving in the real world, but his head is in his dreams by the time that he turns at the corner. Who could he see about this recording? Could he go to the police or the FBI? He can see it all. The man thought that he had power? Well, maybe he was right, but he just handed all of that power over to Harrison. He gave it up the minute he started to threaten him.

Harrison can see the next few months. There will be the investigation and the news reports. Joey will be brought to trial, and Harrison will be there in the witness stand, the terrified but brave man who stood up for the little guy. As they put the handcuffs on a disgraced Joey, Carol will lip the words, "I'm sorry" to Harrison, but Harrison won't have any of it. To hell with her. He just wants his son.

And the thought of his son brings Harrison back to the world. He thinks about his boy and what the next few months are going to be like for him, and Harrison pulls over to the curb and starts to cry for the first time that he can remember. He didn't cry when his father died or when he moved out of the house, but he's crying now, weeping like a child.

When he's done, he plays the recording over one last time watching

13

the traffic coming up from behind him on the left. Right before a semi passes him, he tosses the cell phone on the street, and he watches his blackmail smashed into nothing.

Harrison can't remember the last time he's been drunk either, but he knows that after he has dinner with his son, he's going to drive to the liquor store, then drive to his office, lie down on his couch, and drink until he can sleep.

Deena's Cabin

Harrison finds himself passing Deena's little cabin and then skidding to a stop, way out here on a road that he's surprised was even plowed. When Stanley, Harrison's son, found out that there was going to be snow this weekend, he begged Harrison to take him up to it. Having lived just outside Los Angeles his whole short life, Stanley had never seen snow, but it was a warm storm pushing through, and only the highest elevations had any snow at all. Still, as a divorced father with few custody rights, Harrison finds himself indulging his son as much as he can as part of, he realizes, an ongoing battle over affection with the ex.

So he finds himself here, nearly at the top of the mountain, on a little road that almost no one but people in the forest service know about. "Ah geez," Harrison says, really more to himself than to his son.

"What's wrong?" Stanley's been watching the pine trees all morning. The sun's come out, and it's beginning to melt the snow on the trees, making the it slough off, and every time Stanley see that he yelps a little as though he's been bitten. It's a fascination, but whether he finds it beautiful or terrifying, Harrison doesn't know, and he's learned from long experience that there's no way to know how his son is going to react to something and no point in trying to predict the roulette wheel of his emotions.

"Ah, well, my friend Deena lives there, but the snow plow packed an icy berm in front of her house, and she hasn't dug herself out yet."

Stanley's face seems to be in a turmoil over this, but Harrison realizes that it's just the vocabulary. "Um," Harrison says, "See that wall of snow? I think my friend needs help shoveling it."

"Oh," Stanley says. Harrison worries a moment that there's nowhere to pull over, but then it's a two lane road, and no one's on it today anyway, so he just puts on his hazard lights and gets the shovel out of the back of the truck that he'd brought along in case they were stuck in a drift.

This is what Stanley wanted anyway. He scrambles over the berm

15

while Harrison gets started on the snow. Stanley runs out to the middle of a drift and sinks up to his thighs. He stands in the middle of the blank field blinking at the powder below him and the snow in the trees, and he looks as though he's about to start crying. Oh god, Harrison thinks. He's not going to start again is he. God, don't let him start.

"Hey, Buddy," Harrison calls. "Why don't you try building a snowman?"

Stanley twists around as best he can in the snow and stares at his father. He mouths the word "snowman" as though he needs to lip the word to understand what it means. "All right," he says finally.

And the two of them get to work, Stanley building not just one snowman but three of them standing in a rough triangle facing each other, Harrison destroying the wall that has been put up. He digs out what he can, spreading the snow onto the asphalt, so it will melt, and picking up the ice boulders by hand, tossing them into the bank on the other side of the road.

It's hard work, but he keeps at it steadily, fueled by his son who seems to be finally enjoying himself and the realization that he has about halfway through that Deena's watching him. Since the divorce, there's been something unspoken between them. They stand a little closer. She laughs a little louder at his jokes. Although his job has him roving around all of the California national parks, he finds himself in her ranger station much more often than is necessary. Now, when he looks up, he'll get a flash of her blonde ponytail in the bathroom window, or he'll see her walk past the front door. When he's bent over, he can feel her watching him, and he pulls up an ice boulder the size of a large turkey, feeling like Hercules. That is, like Hercules heading towards middle age and finding himself desperately alone after his labors have driven away the people he loved.

When the berm is cleared, and he is starting on the relatively easy task of clearing the rest of the ten foot driveway, she comes outside onto her porch. She's wearing form fitting ski pants and a red sweater, and she leans against a support beam the way Jessica Lange does in *The Postman Always Rings Twice*. He's not sure that she's making a pop culture reference, but God, it'd be sexier to him if she were.

"Well, thank you," she calls out to him when he's done. "You want to come in and get something warm to drink?"

Harrison smiles. The work, the drive, everything, it was worth it to be here and hear a woman talk to him like that. It'd be worth just about anything in the world to hear a woman talk to him like that again on a regular basis. How long had it been before the divorce that Carol talked to him like that? Years. It had to be years.

"Sure," I'll be up in a minute. He goes out to his truck and tosses the shovel in the back. He's carved out enough space for himself to park next to her on her driveway, and he backs in now, laughing but not exactly sure what's funny.

When he gets out of the cab, he finds that he can't stop smiling. He's going to have to wipe this stupid grin off his face if he doesn't want to look like a complete idiot in this woman's house. He pinches himself and sits quietly a moment. Not too long, but long enough to make himself a little more neutral.

The smile creeps out of him entirely when he sees his son. The boy's body has become tense, and although Harrison can't see his face, he knows that something is coming.

Stanley is standing between two of his snowmen facing the third. He has a stick in his hands as long as he is tall. "Stan," Harrison says, but Stanley doesn't seem to hear him. "Stan, why don't you come in with me and have some hot chocolate?"

But Stanley doesn't turn away from the snowman. He speaks to it in a high pitch voice: "The verdict," he screams, "is heresy! Heresy! Heresy!"

The first time Harrison heard the boy saying something like this, he laughed, charmed by his imagination, but he's learned to fear this moments. Now, Stanley begin to shriek in wild, uncontrollable syllables that seem to be a language all of his own, all the time, he whips the snowman with his stick, and Harrison can hear him start to weep uncontrollably.

"Heresy!" he screams again.

Harrison jogs forward into the snow, "Stan," he calls, again and again as he comes up behind him, but he knows it's pointless. His son has entered that place where no one can find him anymore. He's past responding to words as he slashes the head off his snowman and scores great gashes in the condemned's body.

Harrison comes up behind him carefully, but he still gets a slash in his left cheek from Stanley's wild beating. Eventually, he's able to grab the stick out of his hands, and he pulls the boy close to his body, hugging him although his son is writhing with an energy that he doesn't understand. He pets his head with his free hand and says, "Stanley, it's all right, Buddy. It's okay."

Stanley's weeping now, and his body goes limp, so Harrison picks him up and carries him towards the truck. Deena's up on her porch, not leaning seductively against the post any more, but standing up straight, watching them. He's headed for the truck, but she tells him to come in, and he follows her into the warm house onto a couch, where he's able to sit and hold his crying son. Stanley weeps in loud sobs that lessen gradually as his tight body loosens itself.

After a while, Stanley calms himself as he always does, and he snuggles into Harrison's sweater and closes his eyes. Deena has given him coffee, and there's a hot chocolate for Stanley, but the boy doesn't seem interested. It's for the best anyway. He certainly doesn't need sugar, and Deena's doing her best not to seem disturbed, but Harrison can see the fear in her the way he sees it in everyone who has witnessed a performance like that.

When Stan finally falls asleep and is really out, Harrison lays him flat on the couch, and Deena puts a blanket over him.

"My God," Deena says in the kitchen. "I'd heard he could be a handful, but I had no idea."

"Yeah," Harrison says.

"Is he always like this?"

"No," Harrison says. "He's a good little guy." Deena smiles at him. "He just, I don't know, he does something like that every once in a while. We have him in counseling. He seems to be doing better."

"Ah," she says. "But he's not with you all the time, is he?" She says this hopefully, but as soon as it's out of her mouth, she seems to realize that the question isn't a very nice one to ask. She swallows uncomfortably, but she doesn't need to be uncomfortable. Harrison understands. God, he understands better than anyone else in this world could.

"Well," he says, "I guess you should know that he's around me for as much time as I can get him." He sees her stiffen a little. He didn't mean it to come out as angry as it sounded. He didn't mean anything by it. He just wanted to warn her and let her know what to expect with him, but after he's said what he has and she's said what she has, he knows that whatever was there between them has gone off somewhere else for a while, and maybe it's not coming back.

Maybe they're not going to have a chance, but this evening at least turns into something nice. While Stanley sleeps on the couch, Deena starts to make a stew, and the two of them forget their awkwardness for a while. It's nice, Harrison decides, even now, just to sit here at this table and talk to Deena about their work and their lives while his son is calm in the next room.

The Imaginary Girlfriend

During the appetizers and drinks, Harrison's cell phone vibrates with the ex-wife's number, so he shakes his head and turns it off. He meant to turn it off before dinner of course, and besides, he just saw her an hour ago. She's a woman who just can't say goodbye and leave it at that. After he drops off Stanley after every single visit, she finds reasons to call him and remind him of something that he doesn't need to be reminded of or complain about something that never should have been a big deal to begin with. Tonight though, he's with Glen, his boss, and he told her that it was an important meal for him, so as far as he's concerned, she can wait.

"What kind of money are we talking about?" Harrison asks. He picks up the scotch he's been nursing all night and wets his lips. He takes a sip about every third time that he puts it to his lips, but he pretends to drink every time Glen does.

"Oh, well," Glen says. "This is the forestry service we're talking about. You'll go up one click, but it means more responsibility, and it's the next step, you know." They're in the Buffalo Tavern halfway up the mountain. Why anyone would name a restaurant in California after a buffalo is beyond Harrison, but it's the place a lot of people in the forest service in the area gather after work. It's close for most of them, and it's convenient for Harrison when he's in the Los Angeles area.

Becky, the Buffalo's hostess, puts her hand on Harrison's shoulder. "There's a call for you, Harry."

Harrison turns to her. "It's Carol, right?"

Becky nods.

"Could you tell her that I'm in the middle of an important dinner, and that I'll call her back?"

Glen starts shaking his head to suggest that Harrison can take the call, but Harrison tells him it's just Carol being Carol. Glen knows her from the old days and understands perfectly well enough what that means. He's not willing to sacrifice any more for her. Not one more good thing in his life is going to go away because she's being irrational again.

"Anyway," Glen says. "It's not much more money, but if you want to look at it this way, it's one more rung up the ladder."

Harrison nods. "It makes sense. What kind of duties are we talking about?"

Glen lays the duties out for him. He'll have a team of people working under him, doing basically what Harrison is doing now. He'll be a manager with an office and the ability to affect policy if he wants to.

"An office?" Harrison asks.

"Sure, down the hall from mine."

Glen hasn't said so explicitly yet, but Harrison knows what that means, and he puts down his drink. No need to be chummy now. No need to pretend to drink. An office down the hall from Glen means no more traveling around the state. No more waking up in Yosemite and going to sleep on the coast. Harrison has always loved the travel that is a part of this life. It's the reason he got into the forestry service, and he's never understood anyone who is in the service who didn't want to travel.

Glen leans forward. "Look, what it means is stability like you've never had before." He leans back and grins as though he's giving Harrison a gift, and to most people, this would be the greatest kind of gift, but it's just not what he wants. It never has been.

He's about to tell Glen as much when Becky puts her hand on his shoulder again. "I told her what you said, but she said it's urgent." Becky bites her lip seriously. "I think she really means it."

Glen says, "Take it. You've got the job. Talk to Carol."

Harrison turns on his cell on the way to the bar phone. She called six times after he turned his phone off, and he's tempted to pick up the phone and start yelling, but what if this is the one time when there actually is an emergency. If he's angry, and something really is wrong at her house that only he can take care of, she's never going to let him forget the time that he flew off the handle when she really actually did need him. When he reaches the phone on the bar, he says, "Hello?"

"Harrison," Carol says. There is a desperate sort of pleading in her voice. "Come back, please."

"What's going on?" Glen is ordering again, probably another glass of something, not that Harrison cares or would judge him for drinking. In fact, right now, he feels like joining the man. Now that he knows that he doesn't want the job, there's no real reason to keep his wits about him.

"It's Stanley."

Maybe it is something serious. Generally when she pesters him after he leaves, it isn't about their son. She does what she can to keep Harrison out of his son's life. "What's happened?"

"Did he leave his monkey puppet in your truck?"

Harrison stands at the phone silently, not able to speak, not sure what to say. Glen is flirting with Becky the waitress, and he watches them a moment as they talk. Becky's flipping her hair with her left hand, either actually attracted to Glen or working on a larger tip. He wants to slam down the phone, but he can't seem to make himself do that either.

"Harrison?" her voice is worried. Desperate. "Harrison?"

"Didn't I tell you that this dinner was an important one tonight?"

Now it's Carol's turn to be quiet. He waits a beat and then two. Maybe she hung up the phone, angry that he's not sympathetic with her pain. It wouldn't be the first time she's done that. "I know," she says. Her voice is soft and pained. Perhaps she was just taking time to figure out what vocal tone to have. "And I'm sorry, but Stanley's been crying and crying for the puppet."

"Well, maybe he's gotten too old for dolls. Maybe it's time he spent a night away from them."

She's silent again. Finally, "Look Harrison, you can go out on a date any night of the week. Just this once would you please take time for your son?"

And there it is. That's why she's doing this. He never told her why the dinner was important to him. She just assumed that this was about a woman. She would. "Important" to her equals "romantic," and it wasn't enough that she left him for another man. She's trying to make sure that he never moves on himself. He wonders if she's doing this on purpose or if it's a subconscious thing. If it's not, did she plan this? Did she sit around trying to think of a way to get him away from the imaginary girlfriend? Does her new man have any idea what she's doing?

"Harrison," she says. "Are you still there?"

"Yeah, I'm here. I tell you what. I'll swing by there when I'm done here," he says.

"Fine," she says. "I'll go tell Stanley that he'll get his toy when his daddy is done playing with his girlfriend."

"All right," he says, but he says it into a dead phone. She slammed the thing down.

Back at the table, Glen asks if everything is all right with Carol, and Harrison makes up a story about Stanley forgetting his medication rather than his puppet in his truck. Glen never liked Carol, but Harrison can't stand when Glen runs her down behind her back. He's not sure why really, just that he doesn't like it.

"Well, you'd better get it to him then," Glen says. "But think about the job. Just don't think too long. Anyway, we both know what you're going to say." Glen smiles broadly, and though Harrison's never really liked the man, he feels warmth for him at this moment. Glen is trying to be good to Harrison. He's trying to be a friend.

"I will," he says. Tomorrow, he supposes, he'll have to let the man down. Glen wanted to be a savior to Harrison, who he probably saw as a vaguely lost divorcee down on his luck, and Harrison's going to disappoint him.

Harrison's going to disappoint a lot of people in the next few days -- Glen, by not taking the job, Stanley because no matter how quickly he gets back down to Carol's place, it won't be soon enough, and Carol because he's going to let her think that he was out with another woman. He's going to let her imagination run away with her, and when he gets to her house, he might even tell her the imaginary girlfriend's name.

The Raccoon

When Harrison pulls up to Carol's house at four-thirty in the morning, he sees what he first takes to be a cat sitting on her front porch. When he comes out of the car though and onto her lawn, it stands up on its hind legs to get a better view of Harrison, and he knows that even though they're in the city, it's a raccoon.

"You better take off," he says to it.

It stares at him with its intelligent eyes gleaming in the amber city lights of the pre-dawn, and it comes down on its forelegs, but it doesn't move off the porch. "Seriously," he says as though it can understand him, "get out."

He takes a step forward, and it begins to move slowly off to the side of the house when the door opens, and Joey steps out. "Harrison, what are you *doing?*" He doesn't seem to notice the raccoon that slips off the porch. Harrison steps onto the driveway and watches the critter scamper into the opening under the house. "Har-ri-son," Joey says, emphasizing each syllable as though Harrison were a kid with a limited attention span, "what . . . are . . . you . . . doing?"

"Well, I was telling that raccoon to get off my porch." He hopes that Joey heard the word "my" clearly. He hopes that the man got the message. Until two months ago, he'd been living in that house with his wife and their son. Now, Joey lives there, but it's still Harrison's house legally. He hopes that Joey gets the sub-text that he doesn't think much of a man who has his rent paid by his lover's husband.

"A raccoon?" Joey asks. He goes over to the side of the porch and looks back where Harrison was staring. "I don't see it. You sure it wasn't a cat?" His tone indicates that it's fairly likely that Harrison can't tell a cat from a raccoon even though Harrison is a forest ranger and might be relied on to distinguish one mammal from another.

"Absolutely sure," he says. "He slipped under the house at the loose" he can't think of the word "the screen that's supposed to keep animals from going under the house." This time, his tone is meant to suggest that when he was living at the house, none of those screens were loose. Everything that a man was supposed to take care of was in good repair.

"Yeah, I haven't gotten to that one yet. There have been so many things to fix around here since I moved in that I haven't been able to catch up."

Carol brings Stanley out of the house with the little, brown suitcase that he brings with him when he goes to Harrison's apartment. "Hi, Dad," Stanley says.

"Hey, Son." He says to Carol, "Do you know that raccoons are living in our house?"

"What? I have raccoons in my house?"

"You didn't know?" His voice rising, suggesting that it would take a fairly incompetent person to miss something like that.

"Are you sure it's not just a cat?" she asks. "You know that sometimes you mix things up in your head, and you have a hard time knowing what's real and what's not."

Harrison opens his mouth to speak, but he can't find anything to say in front of his son that won't make his son hate him. He closes his mouth, but opens it again. Nope, he can't say that one either. He closes up.

"Do you mean Grover?" Stanley asks.

"Who's Grover, Baby?" Carol asks.

"He's the raccoon. He moved in right after I started school."

"Wow," Harrison says. "That's very observant of you. You, a young child, have been completely aware of the large mammal living in your house for three weeks while the adults around you haven't taken care of basic house maintenance."

"What?" Stanley asks.

Carol is going to say something, so is Joey. He can see them trying to work out some kind of retort, but they can't seem to come up with anything, and when Carol seems to be starting, Harrison cuts her off by talking to his son. "Kiss your mother goodbye, Stan."

The boy does and runs over to Harrison, who takes his son's suitcase and his hand and leads him to the truck. As Harrison pulls away, Carol is still staring at him, and Joey is looking at the screen that the raccoon knocked aside. Harrison is going to pay for this. She'll find a way to make him pay, but right now, he feels good in a dirty way. He wants to celebrate. He wants to uncork the champagne. He wants to stand on the top of a hill with his son and watch the sun come up over the beautiful world where a little justice does exist.

Bees as Metaphor

Harrison's truck bumps over something he didn't see, and his eyes flit into the rearview to watch his father's beehive come off the bed a couple of inches and slam down again onto the metal. The hive is a manmade box just barely too large for Harrison to carry by himself and painted white. Inside are slats made out of a tightly woven chicken wire and of course, bees and their honey. It's not the honey that his father wants, though. It's the bees and their stings, which are the best treatment that his father knows for his rheumatism.

Harrison's not sure about the idea of a bee cure. He's watched his father stick his left hand into a jar of bees and let them sting him swollen, wincing with a virtuous grimace. It's the kind of pain that the man would enjoy, the kind of pain that would prove to himself and everyone else that he's vital and strong, the kind of pain that tells the world he can stand up to anything that it gives. There's a metaphor somewhere in all of this, but Harrison doesn't know what it is, and he's not sure he has any way to get inside at it.

He's also not sure that he's going to have any bees left by the time he gets to his father's place. When he left, he told himself that he'd just go there slowly, taking the drive easy, and he has been going as slowly as he can, but there's no taking anything easy out here. His father lives off the main road, off any road really, down this dirt trail that no one else drives with the exception of Harrison's mother occasionally. He stops for a moment and looks back. Maybe none will be left when he finally arrives, but they're there now. He can hear them droning in their anger. He can see them swirling around the box in their rage. The windows have been rolled up for nearly a half hour now, the inside of the truck getting warm despite the fact that it's a brisk forty degree November afternoon.

What's going to happen to these bees in a month when the snows come? Surely they can survive the winter, or there'd be no bees anywhere

27

that there's snow, but if these creatures hibernate, what is his father going to do for his rheumatism alone in a cold house, his wife down off the mountain and teaching her classes?

He puts the truck into gear and bounces forward a little. There's nothing for it. The road is rutted from little rivulets that run through it in spring, and it's full of rocks and tree roots, so he just drives the last five miles bouncing along the road. By the time he reaches his father's place, he hasn't lost the hive, and by their angry drone, it's clear that there are still a lot of them left, but they're swirling around the truck, reminding him of a number of horror films from his childhood in the 1970s. Bees, coming up from Mexico, killing people in a horror of a million tiny stings. Those movies were always more horrific than shark or slasher films. He has the image of all those movie bee victims writhing in pain as he drives up to within two hundred yards of his father's house, far enough Harrison hopes, that the bees won't wander in their anger to the house. The man wants to be stung but not that many times.

Harrison considers his options, but there's only one thing he can see for it, and he knows it. He pulls his windbreaker over his head to protect the back of his neck, and he jumps out of the car, running up hill towards his father's two story cabin. He registers that there's smoke coming out of the chimney. He registers the cold. He even notices how nice it smells out here at five thousand feet in amongst the giant redwood trees whose scent fill his lungs, but mostly he's just running and trying not to think of those movie deaths, trying not to listen to the droning behind him.

He hasn't been stung in a hundred yards, so he turns around to pant in the thin, high-altitude air and look back where he came from, realizing that he could have and should have simply put on the bee keeper suit that his father had sent him and that now is resting on the passenger seat. "Where's the suit?" his father asks.

Harrison turns to see the man leaning against his axe. It's a beautiful moment, his father, the retired forestry service man, taking a moment to rest. His once red hair is now white and patchy, his wrinkles have become crevasses, and his knuckles are swollen, but he's vital, still strong enough to split a piece of wood in a single blow. Harrison wishes that he had his camera. If he could take this picture, he'd have a shot of what America could and should be -- this man and the beautiful forest expanding behind him.

28

"I just realized that I should have put it on," Harrison says, "but I'd forgotten it was sitting there next to me. I took it off when I got into the truck and just forgot about it."

His father smiles and comes over to Harrison, putting his arm around his shoulder, and for a moment, he is the man that Harrison remembers from his youth, the unstoppable laughing force that he always knew. "I suppose," he says, "that's natural enough."

The cabin on the inside is clean and well-kept despite the fact that Harrison's mother is down the mountain at the university. She hasn't been here since August. It means that his father is getting better at taking care of things by himself. Harrison's father waves for him to sit down while he makes the coffee. "It'll be a while before the bees are calm enough to move," his father says.

So they sit at the kitchen table and sip coffee and watch the cold day move along. They talk about family. Harrison asks about his mother even though his mother believes in telephones, so he's spoken to her more recently and more often than his father. He asks how it's been to live without his wife for so many months in a row. He asks him about retirement and rheumatism. He asks him about books and the bear population in the area.

Harrison's father asks Harrison about living on his own as well. He ask about the divorce and his work with the forestry service, which is essentially the same job that he used to have, and which has Harrison on his own so often. He asks about how Carol, Harrison's ex-wife, is doing. He asks about Harrison's son, Stanley. Does Stanley seem to be taking the divorce well? What's wrong with him? Well then, has Harrison been taking Stanley to a therapist? Does the therapist think that Harrison and Carol should get back together for the child? No, of course not, but is that the kind of advice the therapist is giving? They aren't medicating the boy for that kind of behavior are they? Well then they're not thinking about hospitalizing him, are they? What does Harrison think is causing him to act out this way? Can Harrison afford to keep up this kind of intensive therapy? Does Harrison need a little help in the way of money?

Harrison's begun to sweat in his pits and his crotch. When he wipes off his forehead with his fingers, his father pushes way from the table. He's been hunched over his coffee all this time leaning forward and listening to Harrison's answers with the zeal only he has. He blinks twice and is out of intense mode. "I've been interrogating you," he says.

Harrison smiles, relieved that it's over.

"I didn't mean to do that," he says. "Listen, I just wanted to know because he's my grandson, but I didn't mean anything by it."

"It's all right. It's perfectly understandable, and you have every right to know those things."

"I don't want you to think that you should get back together with Carol. That'd be a mistake. It'd be a huge mistake."

"Not even for the sake of Stanley?" Harrison asks. Outside the sun has begun to lower a little, filtering a late afternoon light that becomes dappled on the forest floor. There's a metaphor out there, Harrison knows, but for the life of him, he can't get at it.

"No," his father snorts a little laugh. "God no. That's what I did." He pauses a moment in his usual dramatic flair. "Listen, I haven't loved your mother for a good thirty years. Maybe I never loved her, I don't know. We told each other that we were staying together for your good, but you've been out of the house now for twenty years, so you're not the real reason we stayed together. It's not good for some people to stay married, and it's not good for the kids."

"Why did you stay together then?"

His father thinks about it for a moment. "I don't know. I guess it's because I never outright hated her, and it's always been easier. When I was your age . . ." his voice goes away into himself for a moment. "Anyway, I'm glad that you had the courage for divorce. It was the right thing, and I wish that I'd done it when I was your age."

"Are you and Mom thinking about getting divorced now?"

He shakes his head and smiles. "No, God no." He stares at his hands for a moment. "What's the point now? Besides, I like her all right when she's up here, and she's doesn't hate me. When I was young, it was painful, and I always thought that I had to push and make everything in our marriage right."

Harrison leans back in his chair. It's not what he would have expected, but at the same time, he's not exactly surprised. That his father and mother never loved each other -- well that's no surprise. That his father pushed too much when he was young -- that's no surprise either. So much of life is like that, understood but not stated because saying some things out loud is just too difficult.

Anyway, Harrison is thinking these thoughts and others like them, a kind of meditation, as he watches his father put a bee suit over his regular clothing. Harrison's ready to run to the truck and grab his suit too, but his father puts a hand on his shoulder to stop him. His father already has the suit on, and it's easy enough for him to walk out there and walk back with the suit for Harrison. When Harrison is finally covered in the white suit, his father takes the smoker, and they walk out to the truck.

The bees seem to have settled down a bit, and anyway, what does it matter with the suit on. Still, his father is careful to smoke them calm, and they pull the box hive from the back of the truck and carry it on either end. It's heavy with honey and wood, and in twenty or so feet, they place it on the ground. "It's all right," Harrison's father says. "It's not a race. We're in absolutely no hurry."

In a few moments, they pick it up again and carry it a little farther. They do this for as long as it takes, and it's not much longer than it would have taken if they'd pushed it and tried to carry it the whole distance at once. They eventually get it where it's going -- a metal cage specially constructed so that the bears can't get at the honey. It's getting dark here when they put the hive in the cage, and Harrison realizes that there's a metaphor here too. He stands there a moment watching his father and the bees in their cage under the giant redwood tree on a breezy November night right before winter begins, and he just can't seem to pinpoint what the allegory is or what it should be.

He doesn't push it, though. It's enough for now that he's going to have a quiet dinner with his father followed by a long game of chess.

The Christmas Cabin

Harrison is up near the peak when Stanley, his son, asks him one of the dreaded questions: "Dad, is Santa Claus real?"

Harrison keeps his face neutral, but what he wants to do is ball up his left fist and smash the window shield again and again while he screams curse words at his ex-wife. She had something to do with this. She had to have something to do with this. He can smell her in the question. He was wondering if she was going to get revenge, and now he's wondering if this is the revenge or just the beginning of it.

"Why do you ask?"

"Well," Stanley says. Harrison can hear the boy shift in his seat. "Jaiden Morales told me that Santa Claus is just a lie. He's not, is he?"

"Well, what did your mom say?"

"She said that since you know everything, I should ask you."

All right then, this is revenge. Harrison can even hear her tone of voice when she said that he knows everything. She wasn't happy when it was finally decided that Harrison would get Stanley for Christmas. They had negotiated the date, and Harrison had access to a cabin in the woods where they might even get snow, but she had said that a boy should be with a traditional family on Christmas. Harrison had said that he could have had that, but his mother went off and cheated and being alone with his father in the woods might be more traditional than being with his mother and her boyfriend, and that had started up an argument that lasted the whole of November.

In the end, Harrison had won, but now this was her reaching out through her son and getting her revenge. Harrison might have his son for Christmas, but it was going to be a terrible couple of days for the boy.

"Okay," Harrison says. "I'll tell you what. Let me show you."

Harrison pulls over to the side of the deserted road and stops in a clearing in the woods. It might snow tomorrow, but it's clear tonight, and the sun has just set. It's perfect. A damn Christmas miracle. So her plan was to ruin their time together by destroying the magic of Christmas in the boy? All right. Harrison can play that kind of game too.

"What are we going to see?"

Harrison gets out of the truck and lifts his boy down too. He points up at the sky. "I want you to stand here for a moment. We're just going to watch the sky."

Stanley stands straight with his head swiveled back and his mouth open, staring up at the sky. "What are we looking at?"

"Hold on," he says. "It's coming."

Stanley stands quietly for a few minutes, not seeming to notice that they're in the middle of the woods. The dark is nearly complete except that the sky above them is putting on a show. This is a sky that kids in the city never get to see, all the constellations, a crescent moon, falling stars, and what Harrison is looking for, man-made satellites. He would have thought that a kid who had spent most of his life in a city would be impressed to see a night like this, but not Stanley, who is peculiarly single minded. "Dad, is Santa Claus real?" he asks again as though he's asking for the first time.

"Up there," Harrison says. "Right there, do you see that?"

"What?" Stanley says.

"It looks like a star, but it's moving." Harrison picks his son up in his arms, and he points to the satellite weaving its way between all of the other stars. It takes Stanley a moment, but he sees. Harrison can feel the moment that he sees it because the boy's breath catches.

"You see it, don't you?"

"Yeah."

"What do you think it is?" She wants to play games? She wants to get back at him by making her son miserable by destroying the magic for him? Harrison can play that game.

And when Harrison realizes that he's getting back at the ex by setting up his son for an even bigger fall, the anger seeps out of him, and it's replaced by overwhelming guilt. "I don't know," Stanley says breathlessly.

"Do you know what a satellite is?"

Stanley doesn't, and Harrison explains what they are as it speeds across the sky, and he weaves a new kind of mythology for his son. "That's how the idea of Santa Claus started," he says. "People saw satellites in the sky, and some thought they were just stuff that people put up there, but some thought that they were Santa's sleigh."

"Which are they?" Stanley asks.

"I don't know," Harrison says. "What do you think?"

Stanley's quiet a minute. "I don't know," he says, but there's doubt in his voice. The boy's begun to figure it out, but at least this way, it's going to be a little gentler. He's going to ease into the idea, Harrison hopes, and life is going to become a little more bitter, but he's not going to feel so betrayed.

Harrison hopes.

"Let's get going," Harrison says. They get into the truck. There is supposed to be snow for Christmas this year. Maybe that will be magical. The cabin that he's borrowing looks out over the city of Los Angeles too, and that could be special for the boy. Maybe they'll come out on the deck to see the whole city below them twinkling, and though he's lost Santa, the boy won't feel like he's been betrayed, and it's Harrison's fault just in the way that his mother wants.

Harrison hopes.

The Secrets of Crows

Harrison is sitting on the front step of his cabin on day thirty-five of an annual forty-day trip into the back country when a crow bounces up ten feet in front of him. It's because he's been sitting so still, he knows, for so long. He's been doing that, sitting still for long periods of time, for about a week since his reading material ran out.

Before he'd come up for this yearly survey of the water in the back country, he'd become interested in the field of world history -- the study of trends that know no nationality, and in fact often occurred before nations had risen. He'd become fascinated with the subject because of a friend who was finishing his Ph.D. on the idea that cross cultural contacts helped to spur medical advances more than any other force. His friend had fitted him out with a library before he left, one that seemed sufficient for his forty days and nights in the wilderness, but he devoured the books, and since he's finished them, he has been left with nothing but his thoughts, which have been spinning around the big ideas of the universe: free will, objective truth, history -- all as they relate to world history. He has thought his thoughts and spoken to no one for so long now that it seems that there is nothing in his life but this.

So this is the mood he is in when the bird bounces in front of him, and this disposition probably accounts for his sudden desire to throw himself on the bird, to catch the bird, to hunt, in other words, as his ancestors hunted before there were nations or even the most basic technologies, like stone tools. His primal forebears are pushing him to rush forward and grab the bird and eat it.

Before he knows what's happening, he's rising slowly to his feet. Rushing forward and diving would be stupid. The bird would be up and into the safety of the air before Harrison were even standing. He has to do this correctly if he's going to do it at all, so he becomes upright only slowly getting into a stance when the crow has turned its back on Harrison to peck at something on the ground.

He tries to imagine himself back ages ago, hungry, alone, hoping not to starve and knowing that this bird will save him for a while at least. It's the most important thing in the world -- he can't chase it too soon, but he can't wait too long either, else his meal will simply move on.

The critical moment comes. Harrison can see it and knows that it's there. The bird has bounced once again, making its vision of the world bounce around it, confusing it for half a second perhaps, enough time perhaps, and in that moment, Harrison has launched himself towards the crow taking two steps before it seems to notice him, another before it begins to stretch its wings. He takes a fourth and throws himself into the air headfirst towards the only thing in the world that matters anymore.

And Harrison can see his hands stretching out before him. He sees his fingers touch the animal's tail feathers. He's close enough almost to grasp something, but then there he is, sliding on his belly crossing a couple of feet of grass, and turning over to lie on his back, so he can watch the crow fly away. It circles above him once, the crucifix of its body transecting the sun, and then it drifts away. Harrison's meal is lost to him.

Lying on his back, he smiles. He is, of course, glad that he missed the opportunity, glad he isn't feasting at this moment on the living blood of the bird, but he feels that he's being watched. He looks around without bothering to sit up, but he knows what it is. It's not animals or people or even satellites circling above him and spying down on him.

It's his ancestor now, watching him mutely, considering his failure with the crow, wondering what it is that Harrison will do next.

Roger's Secret Truth

Before he left on this trip, Harrison's ex-wife said that Stanley wanted to have the talk. "*The* talk," she said, so now Stanley is bumping along next to Harrison in his forestry truck peering out at the woods unfolding around them, and Harrison is wondering how to have *the* talk.

He had the talk with his own father years ago, but what he remembers primarily was that his father had been so nervous that he'd called sex "rogering." The two of them had crouched down in the garage, and his father had drawn diagrams in the dust on the floor. They'd been stick figures with enormous genitals that had mostly confused Harrison, and Harrison had called sex "rogering" until about the middle of junior high when he was laughed at for using the term.

They come around the corner of the dirt road, and slide to a stop at a place that overlooks a valley. "Look over there," Harrison tells his son. "At the top of that peak."

"You mean at that building?"

"Yeah," he says. "That's where we're headed. It's a fire watch tower."   "People live up there?"

"Sure. All summer long."

Harrison can see the idea of living in the woods all summer long work its way into Stanley's imagination. He stares at the tower, and then the valley that the tower overlooks and then back to the tower again before Harrison drives away.

It's strange how things work their way into kid's heads and memories. What Harrison remembers about that moment with his father is the word "rogering" and how strange and adult it sounded. It was part of a vocabulary of the mysteries that grown up people had and didn't want to let go of, and therefore, it embedded itself into Harrison's memory as nothing else did. Anything might have worked its way into his memory though -- the stick figures, the smell of the garage, the way that his father kept touching the old scar on his cheek -- and he can still remember them, but for some reason, his boyhood imagination really focused itself on the word.

Maybe the fire tower is what Stanley will take away from this trip. Maybe something else. Maybe the whole weekend will disappear from his memory, and the only thing he'll remember about his father was that after a while he moved out, and it won't matter that Harrison didn't want to move out, that he wanted to be with his son if not his wife. All that will matter is that he wasn't there much.

They drive down into the valley, and although they can see the tower through the trees every once in a while, they're still an hour and a half away, so Harrison pulls over and the two of them have lunch sitting on the open tailgate of the truck and staring across a broad meadow.

After sandwiches, Harrison hands Stanley a fruit pie, the kind that comes in a plastic sleeve from convenience stores. It's not his kind of food, but the boy seems to love it. "You mother tells me that you've asked about pregnancy," he says.

Stanley squints and him and tilts his head. "What?"

"Do you want to know where babies come from?"

"Oh," he says, "yeah." But he seems more interested in the pie, which might be a good thing. This might work to Harrison's advantage. Maybe the boy will focus on the food and not listen to him, and he won't have a memory of his father's awkwardness the way that Harrison does.

"Let me tell you how it works," Harrison says, and he gives his son all the details, but he does it as though humans are machines. It's a technical schematic leaving out all of the magic and love and everything that makes men crave love and sex. He's probably too young for any of that, but Harrison knows that's not it. He's being obtuse on purpose, he realizes, because he doesn't want Stanley interested enough to remember any of this, and sure enough, the boy seems to be tuning him out.

He's done explaining just about the moment that Stanley's done with the pie, and the two of them climb back into the cab and drive off. Good then. The boy's staring out the window, and he seems to have forgotten the whole thing. Maybe he's bored Stanley. Maybe he'll have peace, and Stanley will find out the fine details from his friends, the way just about everyone else does.

"Dad," Stanley says. He's breathless, excited.

Harrison stops the car even before he knows why. He can hear that he should from Stanley's tone. Stanley's staring out into the meadow and bouncing up and down in his seat a little, and it takes a moment, but Harrison is able to see what's got him riled up.

Halfway on the edge of the meadow, maybe two hundred yards away, a bear is moving around, crawling over something. "What's he doing?" Stanley asks, and in his whispered question, Harrison can hear magic.

"I don't know," Harrison says.

The bear has a bit of a tree trunk. Some time ago, a crew must have come through here, and cut a log into pieces to clear the road, and now, the bear is fiddling with a barrel sized section, rolling it over, crawling over it, and coming down on the other side only to turn it around and push it the other way.

"It's weird," Stanley says.

"Yeah."

The bear's completely engrossed in whatever it's doing to the point that it doesn't seem even to notice Harrison's truck. It tips the log section on its end, and then knocks it over with a swipe of its paw. "It looks like he's playing with it," Stanley says.

Harrison never would have thought of a bear at play. He's been around them most of his adult life, and he just never thought of them in that way. He knows intellectually that they're capable of play, and he's even seen cubs wrestling, but a grown independent bear playing? No, the idea had just never crossed his mind. "I think you're right," he says.

The two of them watch the bear. Well, Harrison decides, this is going to be the bit that Stanley remembers. He didn't even seem to listen before, and this is big. How many boys get to see a bear playing by itself alone with their dads? Not many. Not many kids ever get out of the city.

They watch the bear for a while until it wanders off, bored with its game, and then they take big breaths, and Harrison starts back up towards the fire tower. "That was great," Harrison says.

"Yeah." Stanley pauses a second. "I just don't get one thing."

"What's that?"

"I mean, you explained how people do it, but why does anyone want to do it? I mean, why would you ever do that?"

A bear, a lemon pie, the woods, and a truck, and the boy is still on sex. "Well, that's hard to explain."

Harrison tries to come up with an explanation, but it really and truly

39

is hard to explain. "I'll tell you what. It doesn't make sense at all."

"What?"

"It's like a lot of things. You know that I like coffee, and you don't. Fish too. It's just one of those things that doesn't make any sense, but as you grow up, you learn to like it. People change, and that's one of the things that changes with you."

Stanley's face tells Harrison that he understands a little, but he still doesn't quite have it. "It's like playing. When I was a kid, I really liked to play, but after a while, I didn't like it anymore."

"Really." The shock in Stanley's voice suggests that the concept is disturbing to him.

"Sure, but playing doesn't make sense either. It's just fun. It's like that with . . ." he takes a breath and almost says "rogering" ". . . sex."

"Oh," Stanley says. He turns back to the forest.

So the awkward sex talk is what the boy is going to take away from this. Fine then. That's all right. Maybe he'll remember some of the rest of it too. Maybe he'll remember the lemon pie the way that Harrison can remember the first pear that he ate, given to him at a refrigerated warehouse that his parents' friend ran. The bear should be there too. Maybe he'll remember the fire tower. In an hour and a half, the boy's going to climb to the top of a fire tower at the top of a peak, and Harrison's going to show him what will look like the whole world spread out before him, miles and miles in every direction. Harrison will tell him how he helps to stop fires, and he'll explain everything the boy is seeing. Maybe that's something Stanley will take with him too.

Harrison in the Museum

Aside from a couple of days for resupplying, Harrison has been alone for the last month, completely cut off from people and society. He's returned from the annual trip into the back country that's required of him for his job with the forestry service, and to his mind, the best part of the year, but the thing is, whenever he returns from these trips, he finds himself fumbling around people, feeling like the awkward teenager he was a long time ago. He's let his beard and hair grow in the last month, and by the tightening of his belt, he knows he's lost a good deal of weight. The weight, the hair, the beard, and probably a hunted look in his eyes force most people to keep their distance, and he's left to himself most of the time.

In the evening, to help himself adjust to the world, he forces himself to go out to a cello performance at the Norton Simon Museum, which they put in the gallery with all of those old European Christs who look surprisingly like he does now, only more benevolent, he supposes. He can't seem to force himself into that room with all of those people. Who was it who said that hell is other people? To avoid that particular brand of hell, when the music begins, Harrison moves into the next gallery and stares at the picture of St. Francis praying for inspiration or forgiveness or illumination or something. It is just Harrison and the guard moving in and out of the room watching him and not watching him the way that they are trained to do, and Harrison loses himself to the cello, letting his eyes unfocus and going into the kind of trace that he was used to doing when he was out there by himself checking the fire watch stations and testing the water in obscure little lakes.

"Sir," someone whispers. Harrison turns to find it's the guard, a forty-something man with large black glasses who's built like a bull, and looks out of place in his blue blazer.

"Yeah?"

"Are you all right?"

Harrison nods and squints at the man. "Sure, just listening to the music and staring at St. Francis there."

"All right." The guard smiles a wavering, thin-lipped smile. Is he worried that this wild man that Harrison has become is going to start chewing on the paintings? And just what was it that Harrison was doing that made the guard confront him? What strange habits has he picked up in the last month that he's unaware of?

Harrison sits down on the nearby bench, but he can't quite make himself concentrate on the music any longer. Before the divorce, Carol helped to ease him back into the world after these trips. It looks as though he's going to have to do it for himself now. And there, coming into the other side of the gallery are two kids who might as well be Carol and Harrison twenty years ago, back when the idea of marriage, let alone divorce, was beyond foreign. Either one seemed impossible, but he'd take her to places like this. That is, places they could get into for free with a student ID.

They ease over to a painting on the other wall, and the boy says something to the girl that makes her giggle. Harrison can see the guard's eyes flitting back and forth between the couple and Harrison. He can feel the frustration in the man, who probably thought there'd be little to do tonight. Harrison's felt that kind of thing before. He'll be in the back country with people he likes well enough, who are well meaning, and they'll do something -- camp in the wrong spot, light a fire when they shouldn't -- and they'll do it innocently enough, and he'll have to become the cop. It's not the job he wants even when he knows it has to be done. Now the guard is gearing himself up for whatever might come today.

The music is haunting, a single cello playing Bach, filling the room with a kind of private intimacy, so it doesn't surprise Harrison much when the two start to kiss. It's what he and Carol would have done in high school or college, and it's natural enough, he supposes.

The guard's face has become resolute and annoyed. When the man started here, did he imagine himself stopping art thieves who lowered themselves on ropes into darkened rooms? Did he see himself thwarting a lunatic who wanted the notoriety that comes with slashing up a Picasso original? Does it chafe on him every day to have to stop kids who kiss and old men with long hair and wild eyes?

More out of sympathy for the guard than the kids, Harrison clears his throat. When the man glances to him, Harrison waves him over. He hesitates a second and then comes over to Harrison, probably because Harrison seems the most likely person in the room to cause a real problem. "Yes, sir," he says.

Harrison likes that. So many people when they use "sir" say it with an ironic intensity that makes it sound like an insult, that makes it obvious that the word is being used only as a matter of form, but this man uses the word so naturally, it feels as though he actually means it.

Harrison leans in towards the man. "I don't know the rules for your job," he whispers, "but those kids aren't bothering me if they aren't bothering you."

The man shifts his weight back on one foot to get a better look at Harrison.

"I mean, why not leave them alone until the end of the song at least?" It's a lot of words to come out of his mouth at once, and Harrison wants to break eye contact, and go back into his own world, but he forces himself to smile a little, and he hopes he doesn't come off as the lascivious old mad man, but as the beneficent adult who understands.

The guard thinks about it, and a smile spreads across his face, and in a moment, the two of them are chuckling. After all, now that the music has started, no one else is likely to walk in. "Do you know anything about this painting?" Harrison asks.

"Sure," the man says. "I've been working here for fifteen years."

"Tell me about it," Harrison says, but he only half listens as the man goes on. He's thinking about his trip. Two days ago, he was up on a ridge, looking down at two coyotes who were chasing a bear away from their den, where they presumably had puppies. They barked that high pitched coyote yap, and the bear sort of moseyed rather than was chased off, but they did it. They pushed the bear away. Two days ago, on that ridge, Harrison was thinking that it was a pretty good metaphor for what love should be and can be or the way that it feels at least at the beginning of the relationship.

Anyway, that's what Harrison is dreaming about while the cellist plays, and the kids make out, and the guard tells him what he's learned in the last fifteen years about art in general and the picture of St. Francis specifically.

The Phone Call

Sitting in his truck outside the convenience store in Weed, California, Harrison is overwhelmed by the joy triggered by a memory, and it takes him a minute, but he realizes that it's the store and the pay phone in an old fashioned phone booth that's done it to him. When he and Carol were first married, they used to make prank phone calls. It was juvenile, but it's what they all had done, their entire circle of friends, when they had been in college, and then when they were married, it was something they could all do that was cheap and fun. They'd have get-togethers where they'd get drunk and call people. The game was to keep the person on the other side on the phone as long as possible, and true masters, like Harrison, would prank call people who had been at those parties the next day, and keep them on the phone in ridiculous conversations.

One night, he and Carol were driving home early from one of those parties, and they called the host of the party, telling him that they were the police, and that there had been complaints about the noise. They almost convinced the host to go downstairs and apologize to the neighbors before he realized who it was. What Harrison remembers most though is standing in the phone booth after they'd hung up and laughing and hugging Carol and how the hug had turned into a kiss and how supremely happy he'd been at that moment.

Later, he'd called Carol pretending to be an ex-boyfriend whose voice was easy for him to imitate. She'd flirted a while, and then when she realized who it was, she said that she'd known all along and that she was just getting him back. Harrison decides that he should have known right then that their marriage would end in divorce. That was one of the signs -- neon, flashing and unmistakable.

On the other hand, he realizes that if they hadn't divorced and that he was with her right now, he would be interpreting their past in a completely different way. That moment would be romanticized. He'd be thinking that she always knew how to play with him, how he never could or really wanted to be able to lie to her.

It starts to rain now, which is no great surprise in Northern California, and Harrison finds himself climbing out of the truck and into the phone booth. He's been thinking a lot about how he should be the bigger person lately. He should call her up right now and do one of the prank phone calls, and they'll laugh about it when it's done and talk about old times, and she'll see that he doesn't have any hard feelings. He doesn't resent her. It wasn't all her, after all. She ended it, but it wasn't all her.

He dials the number and finds out that he doesn't have enough change. He could call her from the cell phone, but she'd just see his caller ID. Caller ID has killed prank phone calls, he supposes. He jogs into the store and gets change from the clerk. Back in the booth, he's a little out of breath and realizes that this has stopped being a spur of the moment lark and has turned into something that's making him queazy. Still, he dials the number his fingers know from muscle memory, and puts in the change the computer voice tells him, and he waits as the phone on the other side rings.

Rule number one for the prank caller, he remembers from all those years ago, is to know what he's going to say, what the prank call is, before he's picked up the phone, but as she picks up on the other side, and says her hello in the singsong way she's had for as long as he's known her, he realizes that he doesn't have a clue what he's going to say. "Hello?" she asks again.

He should pretend to be her ex-boyfriend again and flirt with her. But of course, now he is her ex, and that's exactly what he was going to do - - flirt. The idea of that catches up with him, and he's going to speak, but he can't form the words, and anyway, all of his resentment has formed a fist in his throat.

"Hello?" she says again, this time louder. "Listen, I don't know why you keep doing this, but I want it to stop." She breaths on the other side of the line, and Harrison holds his breath. She'd recognize the sound of his breathing. "Do you hear me, you son of a bitch? Stop calling here." She bangs the phone down.

When she's off the phone, Harrison puts the receiver down and leans against the glass, gasping for air. So maybe he does have hard feelings. Maybe he does resent her. It was all her fault, after all, damn it. It wasn't Harrison who cheated, and damn it, he should have known all those years ago when she thought she was flirting with her ex that she was no good.

What is it that comes up on a caller ID when someone calls from a phone booth? Is she going to know that he's calling from a phone booth in Weed? If she can see that, then she's going to know who called. He has to be the only person she knows who travels to Weed on business on a regular basis. Frankly, he's probably the only person in the world who does that.

And even though the thought alone of doing it makes him sick, he picks up the phone and dials her number again. This time instead of saying "Hello," she says, "What?"

He's almost not able to spit out any words again, but he forces himself to say, "Carol?"

There's a pause on the other side. "Harrison? Was that you a second ago?"

"Yeah, can you hear me?"

"Yes?"

He can hear the edge of ire rising up in her voice, but he can head her off this time. "I could hear you talking on the other side, and I kept answering you, but I must have had a bad connection."

"Oh." He knows her well enough to know what's happening on the other side of the phone. She was all worked up to yell at someone, and when she heard Harrison's voice, she was really going to let him have it, and now she's disappointed because she can't. The anger's working out of her, but she kind of wishes she could have yelled. "Why didn't you just use the cell phone?"

"Do you remember that phone booth we called up Gary from the night of that party?"

"Sure," she says.

"There was this booth sitting out in the rain here in Weed, and I thought I'd call you and talk about old times."

"All right."

In his head, he thought there'd be humor and happiness in their voices, but there's just too much in the way. "So you've been getting hang-ups lately?"

"Yeah," she says. The anger is rising in her voice. "We think it's Joey's ex-wife. She isn't taking her divorce well." Carol goes into the custody fight and her pleas for her husband to come back and now this, phone calls where the other person is silent on the other side. Carol's beginning to become scared. It's just so creepy, but Harrison finds himself siding with Joey's poor wife, of course.

When Carol is done talking about her life, she tells him goodbye without asking about his, and she hangs up. That was always the way in their married life too. Yeah, that prank phone call should have been his signal that she was going to be bad for him. There were a million other signals as well that he would have interpreted differently if she had stayed with him, that he did interpret differently while she was with him, but the basic, fundamental truth, he tells himself in this phone booth that has gone nearly opaque from the steam from his body heat and his breath, is that she flirted when he called her all those years ago. He laughed with her then when they figured out what had happened, but he doesn't think that he's going to be laughing about it tonight, and he's fairly certain that he's made his very last prank phone call.

The Fish Drop

Stanley is awake and up and out of the tent before Harrison can even move in his sleeping bag. Harrison slept outside last night, next to the fire with two sleeping bags zipped up to make one big bag, and he thought that he'd be up with the dawn, but the sun's been rising for a while now. Luckily, Deena's scrunched down a little in the bag, and Harrison can pull the edge up enough so that Stanley doesn't notice her head as he passes by.

"Morning, Dad," he says.

It's funny how many things kids his age miss, but on the other hand, why should he even think to check on what his father is doing, has been doing. "Hey, Buddy," Harrison says. "Would you mind checking on something in the tent for a moment?"

Stanley turns to him with that frustrated look that he gets every once in a while now. He seems to be growing into it. He narrows his eyes at the sleeping bag, and for a worried moment, Harrison thinks he's going to figure out what his father has been doing all night, but he doesn't ask about the extra lump in the bag. "Can I go to the bathroom first?" he asks.

Harrison exhales. "Sure, yeah, of course," and he watches the boy walk out of the campsite, making his way away from the lake to relieve himself in privacy.

"I don't know why you're so paranoid about him finding out about us," Deena says. She climbs out of the bag and pulls on her shorts and a t-shirt. "You're going to tell him eventually, aren't you?"

"Yeah," he says. "I just don't want to confuse him too much. He's been through a lot in the last couple of months, you know. He doesn't need any more."

"I didn't realize that I could be such a burden on him." But she pulls on her shoes quickly, knowing that Harrison wants her out of the camp. As far as Stanley will know, they spent the night alone, father and son out in the woods under the pines, sleeping in the dirt. Sure, there had been other people in camp, but this will have been their special private camping trip. Harrison has his jeans on, and is pulling on a flannel button down shirt to fight the chill of the morning in the mountains, but she's already dressed and walking over to her own camp. "You know Carol doesn't bother to hide her boyfriend, and he seems all right with that," she says.

Deena's right, of course. Carol, his ex-wife, is living with her new boyfriend, who would probably be her husband now if the divorce were final, but Carol isn't exactly the model that he wants for his own behavior. He's going to yell something funny to her as she walks away, but Stanley might hear. Instead, he zips apart the sleeping bags and rolls them up, putting his in his backpack and dropping hers behind a tree on the edge of the camp.

When Stanley comes back, he seems to have forgotten that he was supposed to do something for his father in the tent. Instead, he starts gathering wood to start a new fire. "Not this morning, Buddy," Harrison says. "We're going to have a cold breakfast this morning."

"Oh," Stanley says, and Harrison can see the boy's heart breaking. Sometimes he thinks that making things burn is Stanley's favorite part of camping. He'll sit there watching the flames with the rapt attention of . . . well, of a ten year old boy.

"Remember when I told you there was going to be a surprise on this trip?"

"Yeah?"

"We're going to see it this morning."

As though she's the surprise, Deena pops out of the woods and into their campsite. "Good morning," she calls.

She's waving and smiling, and Stanley waves back. "Deena," he says. There's excitement in his voice, and he goes over and hugs her.

"Did your Dad tell you what's going to happen this morning?" she asks. She's a short woman with a tiny body that Harrison loves and a blonde ponytail.

"No," Stanley said. "He just said there's going to be a surprise."

"Well." She looks at her watch. "If we want to be sure to see it, we'd better go now."

They begin to circle the lake, and as they start, Harrison can see that a lot of people are going in the same direction. These are mostly people who, like him, work for the forestry service and know from looking at the

49

schedule what's going to happen today. It's not so spectacular, but it's really interesting, and a lot of people come year after year, each time with new people following along. "Maybe you ought to tell Stan what we're going to see."

"Hmm?" Harrison says. They've come to a part of the bank where boulders have been piled up by avalanches possibly thousands of years ago. They have to pick their way across them in a dance where they hop from one to the next, never quite pausing, and never able to look up for long enough to know exactly where they are.

"I said that we should probably tell him what's going on today so he understands what he's seeing." In her voice, there is significance as though she's made some kind of profound point that he's supposed to understand on multiple levels.

He wants to roll his eyes or make a gagging motion to her, but instead, he just stops hopping forward. "This is as good a place as any. Why don't you tell him about it?"

They all stop their dance at once and sit down on their own boulders. Deena points to the eastern sky. "I want you to watch there," she says. "In a little while, a plane is going to come over that ridge you see in the distance and fly down really low over this lake."

"Why is it going to do that?"

"They're going to stock the lake. Do you know what that means?" Stanley shakes his head. She brings up her knees to her chest, and Harrison gets the feeling by the way she's sitting close to the boy that she's always wanted children. He wonders if she thought she was getting too old and that Harrison is her last shot. "There are too many fishermen around. Every year, people come up to these lakes and fish so much that there isn't enough fish for anyone else or the bears or anything. They used to bring them by mules up here, but now they dump them out of the back of the plane."

"Wait," Stanley says. His eyes are wide in disbelief. "They're going to drop fish out of that plane."

"Yeah," she says. "Baby fish. I mean, you're not going to be able to see the fish exactly, but they've got a tank of water, and you'll be able to see the water and maybe some little objects in the water. Those will be little baby fish."

Harrison is happy to see that the boy is curious, and he and Deena talk about the fish and why they do it for a while, and as she predicted, the plane, a twin engine propeller deal, comes out of the east. Harrison chose this spot on the west side of the lake because he wanted to be able to see the whole approach, but he realizes now that if the pilot or bombardier over shoot the lake, they're going to be covered in little baby fish, to use Deena's phrase.

He could tell them to move, but he doesn't. He'd rather take the chance to be sure that they can all see the whole thing. The plane dips, heading right towards them, and Stanley shifts nervously, but when the plane just seems to be skimming the treetops, it levels off, and while it's over the lake, a spray of water is released from its steel belly. He sees in the mist, or thinks he sees, little flecks of something, and imagines that they're fingerlings, wriggling up there for a moment, knocking into each other, and for a moment, free in the air, in full sunshine for the first and last times of their lives.

From every side of the lake come hoots from those who had come up here and assembled for this moment specifically, and the sound works its way into Stanley, who picks it up and screams, "Woooooo!" Harrison and Deena cheer too, and without realizing he's doing it, he hugs Deena in front of Stanley and breathes in the rich scent of woman.

Back at the camp a half hour later, Stanley says, "You know, we forgot to have breakfast."

"Oh yeah," Harrison says. "I guess we did."

"Can we have a hot breakfast?"

Harrison knows he's just angling for a fire. "Sure," Harrison says. Fish falling from the sky and now fire. This might be the best day in the boy's short life.

The three of them head out in separate directions to gather wood, but Stanley comes up behind Harrison in a minute. "Dad," he says. "Are you going to ask Deena out?"

"You mean on a date?"

"Yeah," he says. "I think she wants you to. I mean, I think she likes you."

"Would that bother you?"

"No," he says. "Mom goes out with Joey."

He should be happy hearing that Stanley would be all right with him dating, but Harrison feels himself collapse a bit, and he knows what it is.

Stanley had been the easy way out up to now. With Stanley, he could put Deena off and still look like the good guy. He's going to have to be honest now. Either that or he's going to have to date the woman, and she'd be a good woman to date, but God, when he thinks of those last years with Carol, he has absolutely no desire to date anyone seriously ever again.

They go back to the camp, and Stanley has his fire. The three of them are going to stay here today, and Harrison isn't sure what he's going to tell Deena tonight as they lie together under the stars. Maybe he'll put her off and maybe he'll make a decision one way or the other. What he wants though is just to sit with her on the edge of the lake silently and watch the stars reflected in that lake all night and not have to say a word.

Even Puppets Must Die

Harrison realizes he's had one too many margaritas when he tries to stand but falls back down into his chair. Greg and Karen laugh at him and make the inevitable jokes about men who can't hold their liquor while he gets back up, and he's grinning, despite himself. When his shoulder bangs against a pillar on the way to the men's room, the waitress catches him and says, "Whoa, big fella."

In the men's room, his cell phone rings, and because it's the ex, he answers without even zipping up, a leftover act of intimacy. Her voice on the other side is controlled, trying to be fair to him, the way she always tries to be fair with him. "Do you know what's going on with Stanley?" she asks.

"Yeah," he says. "I tried to explain it to you earlier."

"So, what happened?" she asks.

What happened was that as they were driving home from their week-long trip, Stanley, their son, had once again descended into the catatonic silence that he always does at moments of stress. It lasted for about an hour as he sat in the back seat, and when he emerged from it, he picked up a monkey puppet that he'd had on the seat with him and started talking to it.

"I don't want to die," the puppet had said. Stanley's puppet voice was high-pitched and mournful.

"You must die," Stanley said. "All things die."

"Please," the puppet said.

"You are alive, so you must die." His tone invited no debate. He was a judge determined to enforce an unjust law.

"Stanley," Harrison had asked, "are you doing all right, buddy?"

"I don't want Daddy to die," the puppet had said.

"Even he will die. Everything must die," the boy replied.

As usual with Stanley's puppet shows, that was as much of a response as he'd gotten, and though he kept trying to insert himself into the

53

conversation, Stanley and his monkey had become binary stars admitting nothing into their system. Now in the men's room, Harrison zips up. "Is he still talking to his puppet?" he asks.

"Talking to his puppet?" the ex asks. "No. He's sitting on his bed watching his feet."

"Jeez," Harrison says.

"Have you been drinking?"

"A little bit, yeah." Harrison steps out of the bathroom and then outside the restaurant for a moment, so he can talk without the interference of the music. From the outside, he can see his friends talking and leaning into each other the way new lovers do at Mexican restaurants when tequila has replaced inhibition. "I needed something after that week. Look, I would have told you about it, but . . ."

"I know." At the door, she'd said that she didn't want to see him right then, that she had her man over, that this was just the wrong time. "So did something happen on the trip?"

Harrison sits down on a bench and thinks about the trip. They'd been hiking the week of the fish drop. Each year, the forestry service stocks the lakes in the backwoods of California using planes that ease their way into the valleys and open bay doors to drop loads of fingerlings that all fall for an extraordinary moment where they shine in the sunlight that they'll never see again, at least not like that. It's an unimaginably beautiful sight although Harrison can't explain exactly why. He wanted to bring his son there to give him something that his mother and her boyfriend couldn't. The first drop that they saw was perfect. The fish hung in the air for their moment and splashed into the lake like hail. Harrison had sat his son down and talked about the natural world, and how people had ruined the forest in some ways, but that they could bring life back, and now those fish would be fulfilling their destinies. Stanley had stood up from the rock he'd been sitting on and then sat back down, and his legs seemed to wiggle with an energy that he just couldn't contain, and he'd bent over, unlaced his shoes and re-laced them over and over while Harrison was talking. There was so much hope in the little boy's frenetic energy that Harrison had kept it up, saying that people could be like gods if they were just kind and caring and worked hard enough at it, and eventually, Stanley's uncontrollable energy had ebbed, and he'd just sat staring at Harrison while he talked.

At the second lake, either the pilot wasn't paying attention, or the wind shifted, or the fish's destiny was simply to die because when the fish fell from the belly of the plane, Harrison knew immediately that they were going to miss the lake. The water they'd been stored in caught a breeze and was blown onto the glacial rocks on the far side of the lake. The fish were, of course, just fingerlings, but he thought he could hear their bodies slap against the boulders, and by Stanley's tensing shoulders, he knew that the boy could, too.

Stanley had sucked in some air and then had started to charge towards the rocks, his instinct, probably, to be the human god Harrison said he could be if he just cared about things enough, but Harrison caught his son in his arms, pulled him up, and held him as the boy struggled to move and then cried and then just slumped.

Harrison tells all of this to the ex, who, probably thinking that she always tries to be fair with Harrison, tells him that it was nice of him to take the boy, but that he's going to need to up his therapy for a little while.

"That was going to be my suggestion." He can hear himself slurring "suggestion."

"And maybe you ought to just leave him with me for a few months. You know, come by on the weekends but leave him with me."

"What?"

She sighs noisily onto the receiver. "Especially if you've started drinking again."

"Drinking again?" She said it as though there had been a time when he'd drunk a lot, as though he'd been a fall-down alcoholic and had finally gone to AA, and now he was backsliding after years of sobriety.

"You know what I mean."

He tenses his stomach into a fist, and then it occurs to him that if he were to agree with her, he'd have a couple of months off. He wouldn't have to deal with the morbid puppet shows, the catatonia, the anger, the bizarre weeping, or any of it. If he wanted, he could back out completely. It's just a moment, but it's sickeningly tempting.

"No," he says. "I've had a couple of drinks, but I'm not . . . Jesus, what's wrong with you?"

"All right," she says in calm tones. "It was just a thought."

"Yeah, don't have that thought again, all right?"

After they hang up, Harrison stands again and turns to watch Greg and Karen. Greg's feeding a nacho chip to Karen. The nacho is too big. It shatters onto her face and spills onto her, and it's the funniest thing that's ever happened to either of them. It's strange that he can see into their future. He can see their love and their marriage and their family. He can see their child who will someday grow up, too. He will become a man and a father, and then one day, he'll get too old or too sick, and something will fail, and that will be it. He'll die the way the fish died on those rocks, the way that Harrison's love for the ex died, the way that even Stanley will die. He'll die because Stanley was right. Everything must die.

Harrison Dreams of Murder

Before the city council meeting, Harrison sees Joey and thinks of murder. Murder has become a sort of hobby for Harrison. Not just anyone's murder though. Harrison has dreamed of killing Joey ever since Joey moved in with Harrison's ex-wife, Carol and their son, Stanley. He isn't a violent sort of man, but the nature of Harrison's job has him on the road for hours, even days, and there is only so long that he can listen to a book on tape or classic rock and still be entertained.

Inevitably his mind comes back to the fact that his best friend and his wife are living together now, and that Joey is probably going to have more influence on the way his son thinks than he does. Stan will remember that Joey was at his birthday party. If he remembers Harrison at all, it will be that his father took him out for pizza four days after his birthday. Joey will teach Stan how to drive probably, and the difference between right and wrong as though the disloyal bastard would know.

So when Harrison is clipping along down the road, he thinks of killing Joey, and he felt guilty about it at first. Those fantasies were relatively simple. He'd be throttling Joey or strangling him with his tie or beating him with an axe handle (strangely, never a baseball bat), and he'd snap out of it and feel a little sick. Later, he thought about poisons and intricate plots, and even wrote out a plan in his notebook, and just for fun checked the toxicity levels of household products on the Internet. Today, now that he's finally facing Joey as the two of them stand outside the city council in the dark cold of an early December evening, Harrison thinks of holding Joey's head underwater, but seeing the real man wipes away his fantasy a little, and the thought that he wanted harm to come to the man makes him sweat a little.

In a moment, they open the doors, and he and Joey and all the rest of the crowd shuffle into the room. Carol isn't there yet, and neither is Stan, but they will be, and so without talking about it, Joey and Harrison sit in the back row with two seats between them and self-consciously don't look in each other's direction. Harrison is aware that this is exactly the way a ten year old would act if his best friend betrayed him, but he doesn't care. He's earned the right to be a little immature, and he's certainly earned the right to be a little rude. Anyway, Joey started it.

The meeting starts, and Harrison's stomach tightens up a little. Why is it that no matter how important the event is to other people, Carol is always late? Maybe that's the point though. The more important it is to the other person, the later she'll be. She's the type who's always late just so she can make the point that what she's doing is more important that what anyone else is doing. It's funny. Harrison never had these thoughts before she dumped him. On the other hand, Harrison never dreamed of pouring drain cleaner in Joey's coffee before.

Carol shows up eventually after the Pledge of Allegiance and the opening discussion, pulling Stanley behind her. He's in his cub scout uniform and runs up to Harrison to hug him. She's whispering something in Joey's ear in that rushed angry whisper that she has, and Harrison just knows that she's telling him about how someone else made her late. That was what she'd do in Harrison's ear, too.

Frankly, it'd be just as easy to murder them both and more satisfying, too. Drain cleaner would come back to him, and he'd be in jail, but driving down Interstate Five, he realized that all he has to do is put grain alcohol in Joey's beer and then make a couple of toasts. Joey's a drinker, so no one would ever think that his alcohol poisoning was anything but accidental. He could bring some over for Joey and Carol, and leave before they died. One evening and Stanley would come back to him.

Harrison snaps himself out of it to concentrate on the meeting although why he's concentrating on a discussion of water ordinances is beyond him. It takes the city council all of ten minutes to get through that discussion, and they move on to what is for the strange little four-person family, the main event of the night. They call up Stanley and two other kids. The three of them together helped to raise over five thousand dollars for some local hospital. Harrison tunes it out to watch his son who's up there smiling and waving and then distracted by a fat lady with a feather in her hat, but then he's back in the present when everyone starts applauding, and he beams with the other kids who have helped him to raise the money.

When they're done, Stanley runs to Harrison who crouches down and hugs him. He can feel Carol's eyes burning their hatred into his head.

She thinks Stanley should have come to her, and the idea is so satisfying to him, that he smiles and laughs and ruffles his boy's hair.

Outside, they stand facing Harrison over Stanley's head. "Well," Carol says, "I'm glad that you made *this* event at least."

"Have I missed anything? Ever?" he asks.

"Harrison." She uses her tone that's supposed to put him in his place.

"Have I missed anything ever?" he asks, and he says each word singly.

The three of them stare at each other a moment. He's supposed to cower, he knows, but he doesn't. "I suppose not," she says. She rubs her eyes tiredly, and Joey turns away to look at the flag flapping above them.

"All right then," he says. He takes a breath. "I guess that I'll see you on Sunday when I pick up Stanley."

"Bye Dad," Stanley says, and he gives his father a high five.

"See you Stan."

He stands there and watches his son walk away for a moment, and while he's in ear shot, he hears Joey say, "Hey, how would you like me to read you a story tonight before bed?"

"Yeah," Stanley says. His voice rises with his excitement. "And ice cream?"

"Why not?" Joey glances over at him, and Harrison knows he's doing it to make sure that Harrison was watching, to make sure that Harrison understands his place.

Harrison goes to the parking lot and sits in his truck and realizes that Joey has parked across the aisle from him. Joey's let Carol and Stanley in, but he's in the back now, looking through the trunk. Harrison turns on his motor and lights and puts the car in gear.

Murder wouldn't be all that difficult right now. All he needs to do is let go of the brake and press down on the gas. He wouldn't even have to steer. Stanley's wearing his seatbelt, he's sure, and there'd be airbags for Carol, but on the other hand, who gives a damn about Carol? And probably Harrison would go to prison, but maybe he wouldn't. It could be an accident. Accidents happen all the time. So he watches Joey and sweats. He's going to do it. He's sure of it. He's absolutely going to do it.

He anticipates the acceleration and the force and the screams and the desperation in Carol's face and all of the rest of it for a moment, and then when Joey slams the trunk closed and gets into his car and drives away, Harrison puts his truck into park, and he dreams of murder, but his dreams aren't like they were yesterday. They're hard to see clearly now, and they don't make him laugh.

Giving Carol Away

Even from the cab of his truck, Harrison can tell something's gone wrong in his ex-wife's house. It isn't just that Stanley, his son, is sitting on the porch talking to one of his monkey puppets either. Stanley tends to do that in moments of stress -- disappears from reality into a fantasy world populated by talking monkeys. It's not just that. The place feels wrong, but Harrison doesn't exactly know why.

Coming up the sidewalk, he can hear his son's conversation with the red monkey on his hand. Stanley says, "Not every pie is made of eyeballs."

The monkey, in a high-pitched voice, says, "You ate eyeball pie. They told you they were cherries, but they were eyeballs."

"Stan," Harrison says. At moments like these, when something has caused Stanley to retreat into one of his morbid little morality plays, he almost never responds, but Harrison always tries anyway.

"Eyeballs are people. I don't eat people."

"You do eat people," the puppet says. "You are a heretic."

"Stan," Harrison says more firmly.

"You have broken the law that could not be broken." The puppet's voice is commanding. "You are a sinner."

"Stanley!" This time he shouts it.

Stanley comes out of his world slowly. At first, he and the puppet merely stop conversing. Then he blinks and looks around, the puppet going limp and forgotten on his hand. When he finally snaps out of it, he sees his father and smiles. "Hi Dad," he says.

"Hi Stanley." Harrison sits down on the step next to his son's chair. "How you doing, Buddy?"

Stanley clears his throat and smiles. "All right." By the smile and the tone of his voice, Stanley looks perfectly happy, perfectly normal, but Harrison's been through enough of the puppet shows to be drawn in by this.

61

"Really? Everything's all right?"

"Sure."

"Mom's fine?"

"Yeah."

"Joey's fine?"

At the mention of the boy's stepfather, Stanley's eyes tear up a little, and he looks at his puppet.

Harrison nods. He wishes that his son could express himself, but at least the boy didn't say that his stepfather was a heretic. "What's happened?"

Stanley shakes his head, and a little wave of smug rolls over Harrison. Joey has clearly hurt the boy, just as Harrison knew that he would. He should feel anger, he knows, pity for the boy too, but he just feels warm. This was what he knew would happen. This is the result of infidelity, and making Joey the man most present in his son's life instead of Harrison.

"Stan," he says again in a tone that's meant to push the boy.

"It wasn't so bad," he says.

"What happened?"

"He put Mommy in a closet."

Harrison laughs. He doesn't want to do it, but the idea of Carol stuck in a closet appeals to him. His moment of joy, however, is chased away by the flashing anger in Stanley's eyes, and Harrison realizes that Stanley misses Joey. Why shouldn't he, after all? Stanley doesn't understand the politics of sex. Harrison puts on a suitably serious face that he has to fight to keep there as he imagines the ex telling him that she never should have left him for his college buddy, that he had a depth and intelligence that Joey never had, that she never should have cheated and that she should have done whatever it took to keep their marriage going.

"Were the eyeballs delicious?"

"What?" Harrison asks, but he realizes that the boy's gone away again, and that it's likely that Harrison pushed him into his monkey-world when he laughed. He shouldn't have done that. He shouldn't have felt happy that his happened to Carol either, and on further reflection, he knows that he'll feel nothing but chagrin at his joy for her abuse, but he doesn't feel that yet.

He puts his hand on Stanley's head and thinks about trying to pull the boy out of his mask of concentration, but he decides just to leave his son alone. "They were delicious."

"Were they worth the sin of heresy?" He wishes to God that he could get his hands on the person who taught the boy that word.

What good would it do to bring Stanley out into the real world? Anyway, he was able to do that once today. Let that be the victory.

Harrison goes into the house without knocking. He can't seem to force himself to knock. It was, after all, his own house, bought and paid for, even before he met the ex. "Carol," he yells. "Carol."

He finds her in the kitchen doing dishes stiffly, rubbing at a plate in the sink as though she's trying to rub out a birthmark. "A closet?" he asks.

She jumps a little and turns holding her breath. When she realizes who he is, she exhales slowly and loudly. "God, don't sneak up."

"Joey put you in a closet?"

She frowns and cocks her head for a moment. "How did you get Stanley to talk?"

"I just pushed him a little bit."

"That's good, I guess. He hasn't talked in two days now."

"What happened?"

What happened, she tells Harrison, was that Joey had been in his office with Carol and Stanley when he got a call that someone was coming up. "It was a partner for a law firm where he applied."

"He applied for a private practice job?" Harrison's known Joey for years. At one point, Harrison knows, all the man wanted out of life was to work for the D.A.'s office to be the one good man he knew fighting evil -- that's how Joey would put it.

"Well, we discussed it, and we agreed that private practice made more sense. I mean in practical terms."

"Ah," Harrison says. He's been in enough of Carol's discussions to know exactly what it means when someone agrees with her. Harrison once agreed to sell his classic Mustang. He once agreed that he should get a second job so she didn't have to work. He agreed not to have a second child. He hasn't felt pity for the man who took his wife and child before this moment, but he does now.

Stanley, Carol tells him, had been having an episode. Something had happened at school, and no one knows what it was even yet, and in Joey's office, Stanley'd gone catatonic, but only after having taken off his pants. He was standing naked below the waist while the partner was coming up.

"Look," Joey had said, "I can't do this alone. If you can't get him to put his clothes on, stick him in the God damn closet."

Carol had been so shocked that she didn't know how to react, so she'd done exactly what he'd told her to do except she'd gotten in the closet with her son. The two of them stood in there quietly as her husband discussed some of the small details of his employment.

"And you haven't talked to him since, right?"

She stares at Harrison for a moment with a look that is supposed to be withering. "Of course not."

"And this is the end."

"I haven't really had the patience to talk to him yet, but, yeah. Of course it is." Outside, Stanley's puppet voice rises in anger or accusation, and the two of them listen to it for a moment. Harrison's never heard Stanley's puppet so angry before, not even when he and Carol split up. "I swear to God," she says, "it makes me wish that I could just go back."

Harrison stares at her mutely for a second. It was just moments before that he was daydreaming about this happening, what he thinks she's suggesting, but he's not getting the kind of satisfaction that he thought he would out of it. "You mean because I never stuck you in the closet?"

She shrugs. Her mouth has formed into that thin line that she gets when she feels betrayed. "Yeah," she says.

"Does he still keep that fucking bull fighting poster he got in college hanging up in his closet?"

She nods.

"That poster," Harrison says as he shakes his head. Something about that poster sums up Joey so well, defines all of his faults so clearly, but Harrison's not exactly sure how. "Listen, I never stuck you in a closet with a bullfighting poster, but I never quit a job that I liked for one that I didn't like either. Is there any way that he would have gotten that job if the partner had come in and seen Stan's penis hanging out?"

Carol's mouth is a firm line of contention for a moment, but she doesn't argue. "No," she says.

"And he never really wanted that job in the first place, did he?"

"Yeah, he did," she says, but he can hear her doubting herself. She's not a stupid person, and she must have known what Joey was giving up.

Outside, Stanley is saying "Monkeys have rights, damn it. Damn it, damn it, damn it. Monkeys have souls and feeling, and we have rights. You

64

can't eat our eyeballs."

"If it were me," Harrison says, "I'd give the guy a break. I might even apologize."

In all of their years of marriage, Harrison never saw Carol cry, not even once, but she's crying now. He takes the dishtowel out of her hands and puts on the counter and holds her for a little while.

"Listen," Harrison says, "you know that I love you."

"I know," she says. "I love you too."

In a moment, he lets her go and grabs his son's suitcase, the one that she packed. Tonight, he'll spend some time trying to pull his son back into the real world. Tonight, he figures, Carol will call Joey to try to patch things up. He hopes they do too, and that his son has a live-in father finally. He hopes they have every kind of happiness, that they have joy, hell that they get married, and he even fantasizes about giving Carol away at the wedding.

Forest Creatures

When Harrison was a kid, he saw monsters in the forest, and that wasn't a bad thing. He was one of those boys who lived in his head. He loved fantasy novels, and read the DragonLance series again and again. His favorite character was Tanis, a ranger who tracked monsters to their deaths through the forest, and when his father would take him camping, he'd see them there, and he'd follow tracks as well as he could.

At forty-something, he supposes he still sees monsters in the forests, and he wonders if he would have gone into the forestry service if it hadn't been for Tanis and those books. Probably, he would have, but the question's still in his head.

He doesn't know why he's thinking about that tonight. Somehow, when Carol picks up Stanley, his head goes back to his own childhood. He's comparing his life with his son's life, he supposes. It's the little things that shaped who he is today: a character in a novel, imagined monsters that he thought he was tracking through the woods, all sorts of little things. What will shape Stanley's life? The divorce? The fighting? Or more probably all sorts of little things like the snow falling silently tonight, and the kind of thoughts that the quiet snow creates in a boy's head. Tonight it's snowing and they're all, all of them, Stanley, Harrison, Carol, and her boyfriend -- an assistant district attorney down in the valley -- up here, but in separate cabins.

There are more people around -- workers, tourists, and rangers -- tucked in here and there through the national forest, but to Harrison, it's just the four of them and the monsters of his childhood who kept him company. The ex thought it would be nice to pick up her son and have a weekend in the forest that she used to spend so much of her time in. When they were married, she'd come up here with Harrison all the time. Now, as she said the other night, she never gets a chance to go to her favorite spots.

So Harrison is in his home, which is the way he thinks of this forest, and he has at least two guests that he doesn't want, Carol and her boyfriend. Harrison goes out into the night as he always does when it first starts to snow, and walks down to the restaurant that closed two hours ago. The place is quiet now, the way it almost never is, as though nature decided that the traffic and noise that comes with a national forest should be shut down for one night at least, and as he walks, he starts to play the old game again, looking for tracks in the snow. They should be easy to see now that the snow has been dusting on and off.

The tracks are thick in front of the restaurant, but there, clearly enough, is the footprint --two little triangles -- of someone who's been walking through the snow in the forest wearing high heels.

"Jesus," Harrison says.

What's most shocking to him is that there was a time that he found this sort of thing endearing in Carol, and it has to be Carol's footprint because who else would be so vain as to hike through a snowy evening in high heels?

Harrison follows the footprints with his eyes as they lead up and around the side of the restaurant. There's another set with hers, presumably the boyfriend. He knows where she's gone, of course. When they were first married, they used to go back there to the loading dock on snowy nights like this, where there would be a sort of party every night. A group of people who worked up on the mountain, mostly those kids who were just out of college or that age, would get together and drink beer and smoke dope. They haven't met there for years now, and Harrison doesn't think anyone does meet there.

What, is she trying to relive her youth? Out of instinct, Harrison starts to track her. This was what he'd do all those years ago, pretending when he found a footprint that he knew what it was and who it belonged to. He didn't back then, but he does today. He steps lightly and moves slowly because it's important suddenly that she doesn't know he's here.

If he were Tanis from those novels, he'd flit now from tree to tree with an arrow strung, ready to shoot whomever he was following in the chest. The ten year old boy who still lives somewhere in his stomach wants him to do it, but he's too embarrassed to try, and he makes the compromise of walking softly and out of the light.

As he comes around the edge of the building, he smells the marijuana blowing over to him heavily. It's funny. He wouldn't have thought she'd use it any more. Isn't she tired of it? Maybe it was that sort of thing that made her leave him. He stopped liking the things that she enjoyed.

Harrison can see Carol and the boyfriend now, obscured by the snow that's created a sort of mist and keeps falling in his eyes, and obscured too by the trees. They're on the loading dock with their backs to the forest and the driveway that leads up to it. The mercury vapor light has cast them in the stark brightness that creates the deep shadows that are blocking his view of whatever it is they are doing. Harrison stares and cranes and looks to see what they're hunched over, what it is that's sitting on the loading dock that takes so much close scrutiny, and it is not until Carol straightens out and grasps her nose that Harrison realizes she's been snorting cocaine.

It's Harrison's second time tonight to be surprised by Carol. He supposes that it was naive of him to think that an assistant district attorney might draw a line at behavior such as snorting cocaine, but he did think exactly that.

Harrison considers his options, considers popping out of the shadow, considers hiring a lawyer who will attack Carol and her man, considers dragging everything out in court making sure that he has total custody of his son, considers arresting the two of them right now -- after all he has authority up here -- but instead, he finds himself backing out as quietly as he came in. He finds himself keeping away from the footprints and the lights around the restaurant, and the parking lot where there are still a couple of people. He finds himself slipping through the night quietly coming up on the cabin where he knows his son is sleeping by himself.

It doesn't take long, and Harrison watches the house for a moment the way that he had watched his ex-wife and her boyfriend a little while ago. Stanley's nightlight is glowing red in the upstairs bedroom.

Harrison knows he could push the issue. Maybe he could even have the two of them tested for drug use, but he also knows that he's not going to. He knows that by instinct, but when he stops and thinks about it, he knows it's a good idea. He'd never win against the assistant D.A. All he can do is lose. All he can do is push and have the man push back with all of his influence and power, and the only result will be that he'll have less contact with his son. Maybe none at all.

So Harrison, the man, the boy, the ranger, the forest service employee, husband, ex-husband, father, and son, stands outside of his son's window, watching the red glow coming from inside, alone except for the company of Tanis until Carol and her boyfriend come back.

At the Barbershop

Harrison finds himself wondering what human beings are going to evolve into next if they don't all kill themselves before that happens. This is the sort of thing that he thinks of at the barbershop. He doesn't like to talk to the barbers or the other customers, which is fine because they never seem to want to talk to him either, so he sits and tries to read magazines but can't because of the noise, and he thinks his thoughts. He has a copy of *Sports Illustrated* now, and his son who has been forced to sit on the other side of the room because the crowd at the shop left only two seats open, is dangling his legs and looking around him. The place doesn't keep *Highlights Magazine*. No, "Goofus and Gallant" for Stanley, no finding eight things wrong with this picture.

Harrison decides, as the barber calls to him and puts him in the chair, that the next thing humans will be will be less sublime and more animal. It is, he decides, the animal part of humanity that is the best part. It is the animal in people that make them love and care and worry about their kids.

Thinking about parenthood, Harrison checks Stanley in the mirror to find his face transformed. The light of realization and wisdom has filled the boy's face as though one of the archangels came down to reveal to him that the next phase of society is about to begin. Harrison follows the boy's eyes to see that the man next to him is reading an issue of *Playboy Magazine*. So, Harrison wasn't that off the mark. Stanley is receiving illumination, the highest level of illumination that a boy his age is capable of.

Harrison could of course, and probably should, ask the man to put away his masturbatory aid until Harrison's haircut is done, but he doesn't move. He's probably going to have to answer some questions on the way home. Stanley's not at an age where these things will make sense yet. He'll probably have to explain sex along with the confusing realities of the differences between the genders. That much, his curiosity at least, is probably healthy, and this is the kind of place where so many men get their

70

first confusing inklings about sex. It never becomes much less confusing, he thinks. The more he's ever found out, the more deeply confused and even disturbed he's become.

After a while, Stanley gives up the idea of watching furtively, and leans his chin on his fist and just stares. Fine. Good. Don't be embarrassed about your sexuality, Son. Don't ever be ashamed of who you are. Maybe in twenty years, Stanley will be the only human being on the planet not in need of deep therapy for years of sexual repression.

Maybe it is Stanley that all of humanity is becoming. He represents the next phase of human evolution -- unabashedly lusty and animalistic. No pretending that he isn't interested in women. No artifice. No pretense, just a raw reaction to a stimulus the way that any healthy animal would do.

Harrison's not there himself. When his father or mother caught him looking at nudie magazines, they'd hit him. No discussion, no explanation, just a good dose of fear and shame. It's with that in mind that when Harrison gets up and pays that he doesn't yell at the man next to Stanley or tell Stanley he was a pervert for looking or even suggest that he was in any way. If the boy wants to talk, he'll explain. If not, he'll keep his mouth shut, and in fifty years, the people will look for someone to lead them out of the pain of their shame, and all there will be will be Stanley -- the next phase of humanity -- bold, wise, and lusty.

Photography

It's 5:15 in the morning, and the dawn is just coming up through the trees. There's a mist rising from the forest floor that makes everything slightly magical, and Harrison, standing on the ridge pointing it across the valley and the treetops towards the inevitable sunrise feels pretentious and silly. He hiked up here the night before thinking specifically about this shot, getting excited about this shot, daydreaming a scene where people, mostly the ex-wife, looks at the shot, then at him and reappraises him. It had been a pleasant way to dream away an afternoon and evening by himself, but now in the morning, he realizes that this is the shot that amateurs get of the forest, and though he doesn't know what he might be missing, he's sure that he's missing something that the pros would have gotten.

This just his mind torturing him as it always likes to do, he knows. What's so wrong with his pictures looking amateurish after all? He's not a professional, and this is just a hobby. Still, he blushes as he takes the picture, and he knows that when he gets home, he'll delete it out of his files.

What would a professional see here? Maybe the shot that he just took. Maybe that exact one, but it seems to him from the purely artistic pictures that he's seen at galleries and in books that there is always something human in those photos and always something painful.

He turns the camera back towards his own campground to show the fire pit that he didn't use and the tent and the bear box, and he takes another picture in the dull light that comes from pointing his camera away from the sunrise. Maybe this could be symbolic of environmental destruction, but of course, that's just as bad, worse even as an artistic statement, than the landscape. Besides, his camp is typically clean, and the result is that he has a shot that looks like a poorly-lit camping-gear advertisement.

The other camps in the area are less well maintained. Mostly people just dropped their things when they got into camp because they were too worn out from backpacking all day to stow things neatly. Harrison points his camera at the campsite next to his and takes pictures of empty ditty bags and clothing.

The place looks like they came in to camp, and stripped off their clothes in a mad passionate moment where they forgot everything. Harrison doubts that was the case because he was lying there fifty feet away and probably could have been trusted to hear the moaning and screaming that would have inevitably resulted from the sex that the disarray suggests. Still, there's something about seeing a woman's soiled bra, panties, and shorts lying in the dirt that's just to the side of a ditty bag left open in a slatternly yawn that suggests sex.

Maybe this is the shot that the true artist would get. Maybe here is the moment that he should have been looking for. Not environmental disaster, but the close link that humans have to their animal selves.

Harrison takes a step forward towards the campsite and uses his zoom lens. The light is coming up now, falling on the woman's clothes. If he could get the man's clothing in there too, it would be a much better moment. It would speak of . . . well something that can't be said in words, but short of moving the man's jeans and shirt closer, he can't get a clear shot with both in there, and he doesn't want to move anything. His interference might destroy the moment. So instead, he climbs up on a little boulder to get the angle, and he focuses and refocuses getting just enough of the landscape that it's clear what the object is at the same time that it's clear where the object is.

"What are you doing?"

Harrison let' the lens droop and turns to the voice coming up from his left. He saw the man and woman come in last night. She's a blonde, probably twenty-five or so, athletic, the kind of person who never smiles. He was the same, perfect teeth, perfect build, didn't smile. When he'd seen them the night before, Harrison'd made the snap judgment that they were dullards, the types who were so stupid that they were bored all the time hence the frowns. Then he'd felt immediately guilty that he'd thought that.

Harrison steps down off the rock and smiles at her and laughs nervously. "I guess I got a little carried away."

She takes a step forward. She's wearing a red t-shirt and nothing else. Harrison says, "I was taking pictures of the dawn and the forest and everything, but that got boring . . ."

"So you started to take pictures of my underwear?"

The heat is rushing to Harrison's face. "Underwear?" he asks lamely. He's trying to sound shocked, but it's coming off as false, he knows. "I thought it was trash. You know shots of environmental disaster and all of that."

"Yeah," she says. "Sure, how about I find a ranger?"

He's not sure whether or not to tell her that he is the ranger or just to let it go. If she goes and looks for one in the camp, she's going to be looking for a while. He looked around last night. He's the only one here.

"Or maybe," she says, "I should just get my boyfriend." She nods in the direction that she came. What was she doing out in the woods with her boyfriend in just a t-shirt? Then again, he doesn't want to know.

"Look," he says, "I'm sorry. I really did just carried away. I wasn't being weird"

She walks up to him holding out her hand. "Let me see your shots."

"What?"

She comes up close enough to him that he can smell the sweat on her body mixed with a faint scent of baby powder. "If you don't have any weird shots, I'll believe you."

He has a vision of her tossing the camera to the ground and smashing it in retribution, and he doesn't want to surrender it, but on the other hand, what choice does he have. He hands the camera to her.

"Mm hmm," she says. She's scrolling through the images. Aside from the pictures of the landscape he just took, he has some shots of a bear and one of a fallen tree with other new trees growing out of it.

She nods. "All right," she says. She hands it back. "These are pretty good." Her voice rises in surprise.

"Yeah?"

She stares at the viewer critically, nodding her head like an art critic. It's a funny contrast, her serious face with her out in the woods, half clothed and talking to a stranger. If she feels any qualms about it, her face doesn't show them. She says, "I like the bear." She cocks her head. "I kind of feel sorry for him, you know."

They chat about the bear for a couple of minutes, talking seriously about photography. She took a class once, she says, and she thinks his pictures are really good. Harrison takes the praise and smiles, feeling not as good as he thought he would have. This is the dullard after all.

When she stops talking, she goes into her tent, grabs a pack of cigarettes and goes back into the forest the way she came. When she's gone, Harrison packs his backpack as quickly as possible, shoving his things into the pack with no real sense of order. He was going to hike ten miles today, but he's decided on twenty instead. He has no idea which way the couple are going, but he's not going to run the risk of even possibly seeing them again this trip.

As he comes out of the camp ground, he sees his view again, beautiful still, but in a mid-morning sort of way. He wishes that he could photograph this, but even if he had time, he wouldn't enjoy it. He wishes that he could go back and take the shot of the clothing. He wishes he knew what the professional photographer would think of both of those pictures. Most of all, he wishes that he could enjoy any of it, the shot, the forest, or the girl's praise, and he wonders if he is capable of that kind of pleasure.

Harrison's Truck Won't Start

Harrison's first instinct when his truck won't start is to reach for his cell phone. It's probably a good instinct, he decides, but he has the feeling that it isn't going to work. There are a lot of things that he could do right now that won't work. He could check the engine, but since he doesn't know anything about engines, that's not going to work. He could turn the key again, but every time he's done that so far he's gotten the same whirring noise. Just to be sure he turns the key once more, and the whirring sound comes. He could pray, but he's never been on the receiving end of God's mercy as far as he knows.

So Harrison checks his phone, and he is shocked to find that he has one bar. Chances are that he'll be able to contact someone, which is very good news. Snow is coming, and since he's sitting in the only vehicle parked in front of Crescent Meadow, and Crescent Meadow is a good fifteen miles or so from Lodgepole where the next closest vehicle is. Without his phone, he has the options of having a long cold walk, or sleeping here until someone plows out the road maybe in twenty-four hours or so. It's not life or death, Harrison knows, but at this moment, with the storm coming in so hard that it's making noon on the meadow look like twilight, it feels pretty close to that.

So Harrison calls Carl first, his boss who he imagines sitting in his comfortable forestry service office, but as soon as it starts ringing, Harrison realizes that it's Sunday, and Carl won't be in his office. When he gets the man's answering message, he tries to think of who would be in today. All he needs to do is get in touch with someone in the service, and that person can call whoever is in charge of the snow plows today, and they can come for him if they're feeling especially benevolent. But he can't think of who to call, and he realizes that there's really only one person he can be sure will answer her phone.

He sighs and dials his ex-wife's cell phone number. The question, he realizes, is will she put herself out for him even when the stakes for him are as high as they are today. He braces himself for her voice, but to his surprise, it's Stanley, their son, who answers. "Hello?" the boy says. He hasn't exactly mastered phone etiquette yet, so Harrison feels a little pride that he can do it.

"Stanley?" Harrison says. "This is your dad."

"Hi, Dad," he says. His voice rises in excitement. He's still young enough to be excited when his father calls.

"Hey Buddy, I need you to get your mom."

"All right," Stanley says, and Harrison hears him put down the phone and walk away from it. The little guy isn't used to cell phones yet. When Harrison talks to him, he's always on the wall mounted phone in the kitchen that has a cord, and Harrison supposes that he hasn't realized that he can walk around the house with a cell phone.

He hears Stanley calling for his mother. It's a strange thing about cell signals. They're like radio waves. In the mountains, he's gotten stations from Las Vegas and Arizona, hundreds of miles away. It must be that the valleys work as collecting cones for the invisible waves, but they never last. He never gets those stations again. If it is the same thing as radio waves, he might have only a few more seconds until he loses the signal.

The pine trees that line the meadow are beginning to bend back and forth in the growing wind, or maybe that's just Harrison's imagination. It is getting windier out there, isn't it?

"She says she's busy," Stanley says after a few long moments.

"Could you tell her that it's really, really, really important?"

Stanley says, "All right," but he's away from the phone before Harrison can tell him just to take the phone to her.

No, the trees are beginning to sway a bit. The wind is definitely kicking up the way it does before a storm. About a quarter mile from here is an historic cabin made out of a dead and hollowed out giant sequoia tree that someone used a hundred years ago. He toys with the idea of waiting out the storm there. Of course, the truck would be warmer and more comfortable, but he indulges himself in the fantasy of someone calling the ex and telling her that he's frozen to death in a log because she wouldn't pick up the damn phone.

"She says that she's really, really, really busy."

"What's she doing?"

77

"She's taking a nap," Stanley says, "with Joey."

"Really?" Harrison says. "I need you to tell her . . ." he pauses a moment trying to think of what would drag her out of bed with her new boyfriend. What he comes up with is ". . . raspberry pop tart."

Years ago when they began to grow tired of each other, she had come to him with the idea of sex games. She said that if they tried something new and dangerous it would be like they were sleeping with new people. Maybe that should have been a sign to him of where their relationship was headed. He was willing to give it a try, but he'd insisted on a safety word: "Raspberry pop tart."

He'd found the sex disturbing and had never played those games again, but they'd kept the phrase as their catch-all safety word. When someone had gone too far in a fight they'd say it. When someone needed help, they'd say it. No matter who said it or why, they'd always respond.

However, as Stanley puts down the phone and starts running down the hall yelling, "Raspberry pop tart! Raspberry pop tart!" Harrison has the feeling it's not going to work, and just as he thinks that thought, the first snow flake lands on his windshield.

"Oh, God," he says. He turns the key again, and once again, the engine whirrs. It would have been too much to ask the universe, he supposes, to give him a loving wife or a truck that works. Either one was just too much.

"Mom says that Joey hasn't said 'raspberry pop tart' yet so she's not coming to the phone. Maybe in an hour she'll be ready to talk to you."

Harrison digs his teeth into his lip. "Stan," he says. "I want you to repeat something, but you have to get it perfect, okay?"

Stanley must be able to hear something in Harrison's tone because his voice gets quiet and serious. "Okay."

"I want you to say this: 'Seriously, raspberry pop tart. I really need help.'"

"Okay," and Stanley's off again, putting down the phone before he can tell him not to. What the hell, this has become the pattern for the conversation anyway.

That first snow flake melted on his windshield, but they're coming faster now. They all keep melting, but he knows it won't be long before the snowflakes begin to stick on his car and the ground. Up here, they've been known to get twelve feet of snow. Now that doesn't happen often, maybe once every couple of decades, he's guessing, but he's trying to imagine now what that would look like, all that snow above him. How high would the snow be before the light stopped filtering through it? Would he freeze to death or run out of oxygen first?

"Mom says that now she'll call you back in two hours. She says that she's going to make Joey three or four raspberry pop tarts first. She says that they're going to be great."

Harrison pounds his fist down on his dashboard. He wants to curse, and he would, but his son's on the other side of the line, and he wants Stanley's last memory of him not to be as a cursing maniac. "Stanley," he says, "do you remember Sequoia National Park? Remember when I took you there?"

"Yeah," the boys says. His voice is excited at the memory.

"Well, I'm there right now."

"Really?"

"Yep. When you're mom gets up from her nap, would you tell her where I am?"

"Yeah."

"Would you tell her to check the weather reports?"

"Yeah."

"Would you tell her that whatever happens, it's her fault?"

"Yeah."

"Can you remember all of that?"

"Uh huh."

Harrison makes his son repeat all of it a couple of times, but he decides to face the fact that Stanley's probably not going to be able to remember it for an hour or however long she spends with Joey. He says goodbye to his son and clicks off.

He probably wouldn't try to walk it right now, but the idea of being buried under those twelve feet of snow has him feeling claustrophobic in the cab of his truck, and he grabs his backpack and gets out. It's going to be a few hours before he's to the ranger station, but it's better than waiting here. The only comfort he feels as he starts off down the trail is that if he dies out here, his ex, Joey, and Stanley will know that it was all her fault, and that idea's going to ruin her sex life, her new relationship, and the relationship she has with her son for the rest of her life. He's just bitter enough right now that the thought of all that warms him up as he makes his way through the storm.

On the Trail

Harrison's truck breaks down just as the snow storm is hitting, and he decides to go overland rather than follow the road, which would be safer because, he tells himself at first, he knows Sequoia National Park well enough, even if the trails do become a little covered up by the snow. It will probably shave ninety minutes to go directly cross country rather than hiking all the way back to the main road and then curving around following it.

A half hour into the hike, and he realizes that this kind of reasoning is why people die in the woods. David Mamet said that people die in the woods from shame, but that's only half true. Half die of shame and the other half die of arrogance, and now that the snowflakes are finally hitting the ground and sticking rather than hitting the ground and melting, Harrison knows that he might become one of those people who die from arrogance.

The trail here is surprisingly flat for being in the Sierras at least through this section, and although he doesn't exactly feel up to it, he starts to trot, just slowly, letting his momentum do most of the work. Despite the fact that he's wearing a thick bomber jacket and a watch cap, he's not sweating, and he realizes that might not be a good thing. What could the temperature be right now? Twenty? Fifteen?

When he pulls away from himself a little, though, he realizes that this is truly a lovely place. There might be danger, yes, but how many people ever get to see this? It's stupid to be out here, which makes this different and precious. Here, the mountain slants down, and he can see through the trees despite the snow maybe a hundred yards or so. Even though it's about one o'clock, the clouds have made the world unnaturally dark. He likes how the snow makes everything silent. The silence, the dark, the rhythm of his feet, the snow, the cold, and the pines all work together to make the whole experience feel like a dream, and despite himself, he smiles. He shouldn't enjoy this. He really shouldn't, but even though he works in National Parks full time, he doesn't get many moments like this, out alone in the woods.

There should be Jungian symbols out here in his dream. There should be archetypes wandering in and out, giving direction to his life. There should be the totemic animals from vision quests or something. Any one of a number of those animals wander around here regularly, and if he were to see a bear or a coyote or a raven bouncing around, he'd be able to interpret what this experience means.

But of course, he looks around him, up and down the mountain and behind him, and there is nothing. Still, he'll keep a look out. Eventually, the path begins to climb. It's making its way up to the General Sherman tree, one of the world's biggest, and a draw for tourists during the better part of the year, but he knows he's not going to see anyone today.

After a couple hours in his dream, he knows that he's going to live, since the snow is only about four inches deep, and he can be back on the road in a half hour, but he still feels let down. The road will be all right, and maybe someone will come driving by, but he's comfortable here.

In his right jacket pocket, his cell phone rings. He slows down to a walk and takes it out to see that it's the ex-wife. It's kind of surprising that he can even get a signal out here, and if he doesn't answer it now, he's probably not going to be able to in a moment. He could answer it and beg her (despite the differences that they've had) to call someone at the ranger station who could pick him up at the Sherman tree, but he knows he isn't going to do that. He turns the phone off and drops it in his jacket pocket. He picks up the pace and begins jogging again.

Honeymoon

Harrison's telling Stanley a story about a friend of his who is an expert on bats and who explores caves for a living when he sees Deena. He can't believe it at first -- he actually disbelieves that he's seeing her -- thinks his mind must be playing tricks on him, making him see the last woman he made love to, but there she is, in shorts and a tank top despite the fact that it's only about sixty degrees out, leaning against her truck with her arms folded and that look of affected wisdom that she seems to always have lately. When she sees him, she pushes off from her truck and shades her eyes with one hand and waves with the other.

There is no point in waving. It isn't as though he could possibly miss her. Out here, in the Panamint Valley, there are almost no trees, and she's found one of the few hills to park behind. Harrison would have seen her from twenty miles off across the desert floor, had she not parked there, and slowing his truck to a stop, he realizes that was the point. She didn't want him to see her and turn the truck around.

"Deena!" Stanley shouts from the back seat. The boy bounces up to peer over the seat but is stopped by his seat belt. "I didn't know she was going to be here."

"Neither did I," Harrison says.

"Deena!" Stanley shouts again when they stop next to her.

"Hey Stan-Boy," she says. Then more quietly, she says, "Hey Harry. I thought I'd surprise you two."

"Really?" he says. "I didn't know that I even told you I was going to be out here."

"You didn't. You told Glen, and he told me."

Harrison nods. He can't think of anything to say. Anything that he could ask or comment on would sound suspicious or downright mean, so instead they stare at each other for an awkward moment that even Stanley seems to feel. Eventually, she says, "Listen, I thought you might be a little down. And frankly, I had a touch of the wedding blues myself. It's better to be with people when you're down, right?"

Harrison doesn't answer the question, but tells her to follow him, that he has a spot already in mind to stop for the night, up the side of the mountain. She smiles her wan smile, and they drive down the road in single file. In the rearview, he can see her beaming proudly at what she's done.

He is almost happy to see her, and she's right: He should be with someone his own age this weekend. His wife, his ex-wife, is on her honeymoon now. That would have been bad enough, but Harrison has been acting like an adult for so many straight hours now that he's just about ready to throw a tantrum. He wants to stop the truck and walk to the middle of the dirt road and scream and scream and scream. He's been wanting to do that all week, but he's been restraining himself for the sake of Stanley and because he's an adult.

The wedding had become much worse for him a week ago when the ex had called and told him that her parents had opted out of the wedding. Those were her words "opted out." This didn't surprise Harrison. Her parents had always been conservative when it came to things like wedding vows, and they were dramatic in exactly the same way the ex was. At the last moment, her father had called and said that he refused to walk her down the aisle, that what she was doing was adulterous, and he'd have no part in it.

The ex's brilliant idea was to get Harrison to walk her down the aisle instead. "Come on," she'd said. "You can't still be hung up on me." He snickered at that with her as though she were actually being funny. "Be an adult. Besides, it'll be good for Stanley to see that you aren't upset by the whole thing."

And so, of course, after that, he had to walk her down the aisle, the one final act proving that she had won the divorce.

So Deena was right. He probably shouldn't be alone right now, but seeing her behind him singing along to whatever CD she's listening to, he feels trapped the way he felt trapped in those final months before he moved out of the ex's house.

They come to a road that branches off from their dirt road and goes straight up the mountain. Harrison keeps an eye on Deena as often as he can as they go up the cliff face, but she seems undaunted by the thousands of feet straight off to their left. She's smiling and singing along with her music still even as Harrison can't seem to allow himself to breathe deeply. This was a road built, what, a hundred years ago? And it was built for miners driving horses and buck boards, not heavy steel trucks. He's been up here before and knows others who've made the drive, but that's not making him any less nervous, and he wonders if he'd turn around without her here.

Eventually, the road widens out to a deck at the top of the mountain, and they park side by side and get out, setting up camp behind the trucks. Deena's taken care of dinner, she says, and has "her men" set up the tents while she heats up the food. When Harrison puts up her tent, she says, "Just throw your sleeping bag in there next to mine." She stares at him hard with her affected wisdom.

Dinner consists of Stanley's favorites. Somehow on a camp stove, she's reheated pizza from Stanley's favorite pizza parlor. There is root beer for him and bourbon for them. For dessert, she's transported something that she and Stanley developed once together without consulting Harrison - - vanilla Oreos with whipped cream and honey. The flavor is cloying, and Harrison cannot imagine that anyone but a kid would actually like it, but the two of them exclaim over it as Harrison watches and sips his liquor.

Eventually, Stanley goes into the tent, and Deena and Harrison sit cross-legged on a blanket near the cliff's edge and watch the satellites passing overhead and the bats flitting around them. They're silent for a long time, but Harrison breaks the silence. "You know, it was nice of you to bring stuff for Stan, but you can't feed kids that kind of food. It's not good for them."

"It's fine," she says. "It's not every day, and he needs a little TLC this weekend of all weekends."

"He's doing all right," Harrison says, and he's about to continue when she cuts him off.

"He's not doing all right. He needs a woman in his life. I mean . . . Harrison, you can't see how much he's hurting because you're hurting too." Her voice is feminine and full of understanding. "I don't think you are capable of understanding how much pain you're in right now. You had to be crazy to come up here by yourself like that."

"Deena," he says, but he doesn't know how to express what he's feeling for her. He's not even sure what it is that he's feeling, so when she leans in and kisses him, he simply kisses her back. She's wrong. He knows exactly how much he's hurting, and he knows that this is possibly the worst choice he can make, but he makes it. He kisses her back, taking her head in his hand. He makes love to her there, under the stars and above the desert.

Afterwards, they lie in the dark side by side, and he says, "You can't surprise us like this any longer. I need to be in control of my son's life." "All right, my love," she says in a sing-song, and he wishes that she'd told him no, that she was going to do whatever she wanted, so he could yell at her. It would have been the excuse he needed to end the thing, and he could dwell on the fact that it's going to be that much harder to end the relationship now, and maybe he could tell her how he's feeling and that she needs to go slower with him or possibly leave him alone, but doing that would be the adult thing to do, and he's so damn tired of being the adult.

In the morning, Deena makes a show of asking Harrison what Stanley should have for breakfast, and cooks the eggs and slices up the fruit obligingly humming a tune from *Cabaret* and smiling the whole time. They'd slept on the edge of the cliff in their sleeping bags, waking up in the morning before the stars had all gone out and had made love in the bluing light.

He's never seen her more happy, and he wonders if she thinks that like the ex, she's won the divorce too. When Stanley comes out in his little-boy pajamas rubbing his eyes, she smiles at him and says, "How's my little man?" She hugs him and tickles him when he comes in close, and he tells her to stop, but he clearly likes the attention. Harrison smiles at the whole scene despite himself. He's not going to frown. He's not going to be the adult. He's going to enjoy whatever it is that life gives him right now without thinking about what the future might look like.

When breakfast is done, and the three of them have cleaned the dishes, she says, "What's the plan for today?"

"Well," Harrison says, "I was going to show Stanley some of the old mines up here."

"You're going to go into the mines?" She's asking Stanley really, and her voice rises up with contrived excitement tinged with fear. "You're going into those old shafts?"

"Not far," Harrison says, "and not into any that are dangerous."

"Still," she says to the boy, "you have to be pretty brave to do that. And you'd better be wearing your blue jeans." Stanley gets the point and runs off to get dressed as she watches him with a maternal head cock. "He's a great kid, isn't he?"

Harrison wants to ask if she realizes that he isn't her kid, but he lets it go. He's going to make love to her again tonight. It's just easier this way. "Yeah," Harrison says. "He got a book on bats last month, and he's been talking about nothing else non-stop."

She shrugs. "It's his way of dealing, you know?"

"I know," he says although he doesn't know. In fact, he's pretty sure that the boy has other coping methods that she's never seen, but this is a lot easier.

Stanley comes out eventually in his jeans, a jeans jacket and a backpack. She buttons the jacket up for him, and they start down the trail towards the mine shaft, Harrison and Deena walking on either side of his son. Harrison can see the mine opening a good half mile away. Stanley can't see it at first, and neither can Deena, but Harrison tells them that from a long way off, they should look for the dump, not the hole in the mountain. "Sometimes the hole is at a weird angle, but just below the entrance is a massive pile of dirt and ore that's been dug out. Do you see it?"

The two of them nod and Deena watches Stanley with maternal pride as he figures out what he's looking at. "The general rule of thumb," Harrison says, "is the bigger the dump, the bigger the mine. That's usually true out in the desert, but sometimes the dump disappears for one reason or another."

By the size of the dump, which flows glacially down the V of the valley, this is a fairly large mine, but that doesn't matter too much. It's not as though they're going to risk going into the depths of the earth to find artifacts from a hundred years ago. People disappear that way. People die that way. Harrison just wants to take his son twenty feet in.

When they reach the entrance, however, Deena asks, "Do you think this is safe?"

Harrison points his flashlight at the floor of the shaft. "It should be safe enough for us. There's no rocks on the ground which means that the mine isn't crumbling. The important thing is to remember to crouch until I tell you it's safe. Don't ever allow your head to touch the ceiling or come even close."

"Why not?"

"Trust me on this one."

The shaft is about five feet high, which means that Deena and

Harrison have to bend at the waist, and they bend their knees too, giving themselves a good two feet of clearance. Stanley could stand upright without a problem, but he imitates the adults as they all walk into the mine, Harrison first, then Stanley, then Deena.

Twenty-five feet in, Harrison stops and comes down on his haunches. He holds Stanley around the waist and turns him towards the entrance, and Deena crouches next to them too. "Okay Stan, do you remember what your book said about bats?"

"Yeah?"

"What do they do in the day time?"

"They go someplace where it's dark all the time." That's a direct quotation from his book.

"Places like caves," Harrison says. Harrison's flashlight is pointed at the ground, but he brings it about halfway up the tunnel wall. "I don't want to put my light directly on the roof, but look up there."

In the reflected light, the ceiling seems to be wriggling a little in clumps. Here and there are dark circles hanging three inches off the rock, moving like independent blobs, and he wonders what it is that Stan is seeing, how his mind is making sense of all of this.

"What is it?"

"When bats sleep," Harrison says, "they get together in little clusters for protection. One or two stay awake, but the rest hang from their feet and sleep the day away in a place just like this one. What you're seeing is a big bat city with almost everyone asleep."

"Oh," Stanley says.

"Jesus Christ," Deena says.

As his eyes adjust to the light of the cave, Harrison begins to make out the bats. The bat cluster is both individuals and a single animal at the moment. There is individual movement as bats adjust in their sleep, but the cluster seems to sway back and forth together as a unit as though there is a blustery wind in this breezeless cave.

Harrison can feel his son's body stiffen in excitement as he watches the whole scene, and he can sense the kid becoming a scientist in his arms at this moment. If, in twenty years, the boy graduates with a Ph.D. in something, Harrison knows that he'll trace his interest in the natural world back to this moment, right now, and he crouches silently afraid to move and upset the beauty and wonder for the boy in this moment.

"I gotta get a picture of this," Deena says next to him. Before Harrison can register what she's said, before he can stop her, she lifts her disposable camera and clicks the button, turning the dark of the cave into daylight with the cold bluish light of the flash.

Harrison gasps a little, silently, and since he is holding Stanley, the boy tenses too. Harrison doesn't know much about bats, not enough to know how they're going to react, but he knows what's going to happen to Stanley if the bats are startled awake *en masse* by the light and start flying around chaotically brushing up against the boy, getting into his hair, as the three of them run screaming into the sunlight.

"That's great," Deena says, and Harrison wants to grab the camera out of her hand and crush it under his foot, and by the time he has that thought, and he realizes that she's winding the film, he also realizes that the bats haven't woken up. They're still up there swaying back and forth in a stiff breeze that doesn't exist.

"It's okay," Harrison says to himself.

"So what do you think, Stan-Boy?"

Stanley's silent a moment. "It's cool," he says finally, and to Harrison's relief, there's a dreamy sort of wonder in his voice.

Eventually, the three of them exit the cave and sit on boulders at the top of the dump. Harrison tells Stanley all of the bat science that he knows, which isn't much. He tells him about the old miners who came out here to find minerals and how hard that life was. He tells the boy that they liked the bats because gases that kill people can be released deep in the earth, and as long as the bats are there and still alive, the people know that they'll be all right. He's not entirely sure about that one, but he says it anyway because the boy is sitting there with his childish intensity looking up at his father in wonder and admiration, and Harrison needs to keep the conversation going.

They go back in every once in a while to look at the animals for a moment, and then walk out to talk about them. They're beautiful and disgusting at once, and they keep the three of them occupied until lunch. At lunch, they walk back with Stanley, who is running up ahead of them checking out rocks on the path.

"Well, what are you going to do as an encore to that?" Deena asks. "Do you have a viper pit or something?"

Harrison laughs. "No, tomorrow, I was planning to go to the other side of this mountain range. There's a couple of ghost towns over there that no one gets to."

"A real live ghost town. Stanley's never going to forget that."

"That's the idea."

"He's never going to forget those bats either. I'm going to have that picture blown up into a poster for him." She kisses Harrison on the cheek. "Thank you so much for bringing me up here." And although he didn't exactly bring her, he smiles and kisses her back. "I thought for sure that flash was going to wake those bats up."

"So did I."

"I'm so sorry that it didn't. I was about to throw a rock at them to stir them, but I realized how cruel that would have been."

"You wanted to wake them up?"

"Yeah, could you imagine all of those bats fluttering all around us. They would've been kind of dancing with us. Now that would have made a great picture."

Harrison doesn't know what to say to this, so he keeps his mouth closed. What is there to say? He either has to agree with her, and the idea of those bats flapping around him makes him physically sick, or he has to break up with her right now, tell her how stupid that was, how it nearly ruined what he was trying to do for his son. He'd need to tell her that she's suffocating him at the exact wrong moment, and that he needs time to work out his feelings, that he just gave his wife away, the woman he still loves, to the man she had an affair with. He'd need to tell her that he needs space, and that even though she's probably too old to have children herself, she can't make Stanley into her son. But all of that would be the adult thing to do, so he keeps his mouth shut, hoping that they'll make love two or three times again tonight.

In the morning, Harrison finds himself standing on the valley floor with Stanley saying goodbye to Deena. "Can't you come with us?" Stanley asks.

"Sorry, Stan-Boy, I've got to get back to work. But when you get back, make sure to come see me." She tousles Stan's hair, and leans into Harrison to kiss him on the cheek. "You be sure to come to see me too. I want to see you the moment you're back in L.A."

Harrison doesn't respond exactly. He grunts noncommittally the way teenage boys do. He and Stan climb back into the truck, but Deena stands outside, arms folded and leaning up against her door. She waves at them the way she did when they drove up, and Harrison watches her in his rearview as long as he can, but she doesn't seem to want to leave this place ever, and she stays leaning against her truck, with that affected wisdom on her face until she disappears behind the hill.

The Aqueduct

Harrison and Deena can see water sloshing over the edge of the aqueduct in a spray that comes down on the road. The spray would be dangerous except at this time of year, almost no one drives this road. There will be snow up ahead, and they've been in and out of fog patches all day. It's an aluminum sluice built as part of the WPA, running on the side of the mountain through the trees, just above the road. It's held up by a wooden structure that has been dark brown with age since Harrison was a kid and his father took him up here, and when he thinks about it, he realizes that it's kind of amazing that it needs so little maintenance.

It needs maintenance now though. He can see that from here, from his forestry service truck. Deena's been out here more than he has, and she knows the aqueduct better than he does. "There's a maintenance point just ahead," she says. Harrison slows the truck and pulls into the dirt parking spot that's probably been there since FDR's time too.

Deena's already up the ladder and onto the top of the aqueduct while Harrison's getting out his camera. He bought an expensive camera and a computer to go with it a couple of months after his divorce, and his pictures and dreams of a professional side career, he realizes, are a part of his need to sublimate his sexual impulses, but that knowledge hasn't seemed to dampen his enthusiasm for it at all. It makes sense for him to take pictures, anyway. He's up and down California in national parks all the time, seeing things that other people have no idea exist, and here he can see that they might have a great view of the road winding up the foothills, maybe in and out of the fog. He only hopes that Deena doesn't start vamping for the camera again.

He climbs up heavily and stands behind Deena. They're standing on two by fours that go the length of the aqueduct, and under the boards, the water flows. It's an interesting system, two two by fours next to each other creating a permanent path for access, but they feel flimsy under his feet.

Deena bounces on them a minute, and they groan under her light weight. She smiles when she sees his camera. "Take a picture of me," she says and bounces again. She leans seductively against the handrail and blows him a kiss.

Harrison smiles and obeys, clicking the shot that he'll discard later. "I love that camera of yours," she says.

"Yeah, I noticed." He's taken hundreds of pictures of her. He could wallpaper his house with the pictures he's taken of her. It brings out the flirt in her, and every time he's pulled it out, she's started to pose seductively. Now, that he's taken the picture, she come up close to him.

"Let me see it," she says. She hugs his arm and looks down at the digital display.

But her quick movement has thrown him off balance and the two of them lean backwards, and the board beneath them groans, and Harrison moves his leg to regain balance, but he steps into the snow runoff beneath him, and he's going to go in and be dragged by the freezing sluice all the way down twenty or more miles into the reservoir, but he catches himself on the handrail, and thank God for camera straps because he had to let go of the camera to grab the rail.

"Oh God," she says, and she tries to grab him, but misses, and she has to catch herself too. When they're finally righted, he knows that he's going to break up with her and pretty soon too. He knows that he's known deep down for a long while, but he just hasn't been able to work himself up to the final confrontation. He's always hated confrontation. It's one of the reasons he went into forestry work in the first place. He had the misguided notion that he'd be free of all of that, and that he'd work alone way out in the forest.

She laughs. "I guess I should keep my distance until we're off this thing."

"Yeah, I guess so," he says, and he tries his best to sound rueful. She turns and walks downhill, picking up the kind of pace she's capable of. She's athletic after all, and used to hiking at this altitude and higher, and she's fearless, bouncing on the boards and not holding onto the handrails the way any other woman would. Hell, any other man would too. She's not a terrible person. He even has affection for her. He likes her a lot, but he can't stand being with her all the time any longer.

"Wait," she says. She spins around, and strikes a dramatic pose.

Harrison lifts the camera instinctually and takes the shot. When she hears the artificial click that the digital camera makes, she giggles and goes off again.

Maybe it's her constant need for attention, his attention, that he's sick of. If he could have a little time off from her, it'd be a lot easier to be her boyfriend. She's pushing for marriage even now, and his divorce isn't anywhere near complete yet.

They come to the water spray. A branch got lodged into the aqueduct somehow, and it's created a sort of dam. All the little bits that flowed down it have been caught, but it takes only a few minutes to clear it all out, throwing the bits over the left side because the road's running beneath them to the right.

When they're done, Harrison has his moment to take pictures. He shoots the mountain across the canyon and tries to get a shot of the road coming up here. It's not what he imagined though. There's no dramatic vista, and in fact, the most interesting bit is the aqueduct. He takes ten or eleven shots of it: close ups of details, shots of the water below, a shot of the board walkway running up the middle. The view of the mountains isn't great, but he imagines this walkway at different times. There's been fog moving through these mountains all day. Would there be a mystical flavor to the scene -- the walkway, suspended thirty feet off the ground in fog? Maybe not, but he'd be willing to wait to see, and he wonders if Deena would wait with him.

This is what he's thinking about when something hits him on the back.

He turns around to find Deena laughing. The thing she threw was her shoe, and it's lying on the board at his feet now.

Without thinking about it, he kicks it, just touches it, really, meaning to knock it to the right into the road below them, but he doesn't put enough force behind it and instead, it tumbles into the water beneath them, and just like that, it's gone, swept away. He's all ready to apologize, but she feigns indignant surprise and squeaks and laughs. "Take my picture," she says.

He lifts the camera and starts to shoot. She takes off her other shoes and drops it in the sluice. Then she takes off her socks, and they follow. She's wearing just a light jacket, but she takes it off and her jeans and her flannel shirt, all the time undulating just a little, humming a song that's vaguely burlesque. Each piece she strips off, she drops into the water which sweeps it away forever. When she's down to her bra and panties, she turns away from him, strips them off and throws them high into the air, where they catch a breeze and flutter like pink leaves onto the road below them.

"You're out of your mind," he says.

"Shut up and take my picture," she says. "Do you want me?" She has that crazy energy that takes her over sometimes, and it's pulsing in her eyes now, and he thinks that half of it is the fact that a car could come down the road at any moment. She's not going to want to sit here quietly waiting for a shot.

He says that he does want her because it seems to be the polite thing to do, but frankly, he'd rather stand here waiting for the fog to roll in. She's getting something out of this dance, but he isn't. The real truth is that she's bugging the shit out of him. All he can think about is how cold she must be standing up here without any clothes on, and what a hassle it's going to be to find new clothes for her in her suitcase in the truck.

What he really wants is to tell her, right here and now that he's got to break up with her, that watching her strip down up here was the least sexy and most desperate thing that he ever saw, but again, it seems a little impolite to do, and even if he did, he couldn't just stand up here alone waiting for the shot like he wants to.

Photography is an ephemeral thing. If he misses the moment, the shot will be gone forever, and he's going to miss something amazing here, he just knows it, but he's not going to miss another shot again, not because of her, at least. He'll stay with her a while, probably until the end of their weekend together, but he makes a vow now that he's not going to lie any longer after that, and that when she's gone, he's never going to waste his time with someone like her again.

The Hitchhiker

Harrison doesn't pick up hitchhikers as a rule, not since the eighties when he was young and stupid enough to think that it was the kind thing to do. Also, he's not supposed to when he's in his uniform and driving a national park vehicle. He knows there's a rule about that somewhere, and if there isn't, there should be, but when he comes up behind her, she looks so tiny that he watches her from his rearview after he passes. Maybe it's a trick of the mirror, but she looks like a kid. She could be in her twenties and look young, but he thinks she's probably closer to sixteen. She's a good forty miles from the highway and coming out of the back country with a fully-loaded pack. He slides to a stop because almost no one comes out here, but he has a waking nightmare that the next person down the road will stop for her, and no one will ever hear from this girl again.

"Hello," she says, and he can't identify it from just one word, but she has an accent. "Thank you for stopping. I haven't seen anyone on this road."

German, he thinks. She has a German accent. "No," he says. "No one drives out here except for backpackers, and it's still a little early in the season yet." No, no one but people in the forestry service and backpackers except the occasional illegal hunter. Maybe teenagers looking for a private place to drink. A survivalist now and then. Druggies. Mob guys dumping bodies.

"Oh," she says. "Who's that?"

She's swinging into the truck now, staring into the back seat where Harrison's son is curled up asleep under a blanket. "That's Stanley," he says. "I'm Harrison."

"Kirsten," she says, and she shakes his hand. She's probably closer to nineteen or twenty, he decides, blonde ponytail, and a light blue tank top that doesn't quite hide her belly button piercing.

*   *   *

Kirsten reminds him of the last German he met, the last one he can remember, anyway. That was another kid who needed help, this one a boy about six years old. Harrison had been in Sears and saw the little black-haired child with the bowl cut and suit turning around in circles looking for something. Harrison might have gone to the sales people, but they were clearly inundated, and besides they'd seemed slow witted when he'd bought his boots. There was a photographer in the store, he thought he remembered, and the way the boy was dressed, he assumed that he must be looking for that.

"Are you lost?" he'd asked the boy.

The boy had said something and then repeated himself when Harrison only blinked. It had been nearly ten years since he'd taken his last German class, but Harrison had recognized that the child was speaking German even though he wasn't sure at all what the boy had said.

"*Bist du Eltern gehen?*" Harrison had said. It had been a long time, but he knew that was wrong. He'd wanted to ask the boy where his parents had gone, but either the words or his accent were off because the boy just looked at him. "*Sprechen sie Englisch?*"

That much he thought at least made sense, but the boy said, "*Nein.*"

Harrison gestured for the boy to stay where he was, and he stood on tiptoes casting about for concerned-looking adults. When he saw no one, he did his best to tell the boy that he'd help him find his parents, but the boy just looked confused and started to sob.

*   *   *

Kirsten has been in the high country by herself for about a week.

"Weren't you cold?" Harrison asks. "Didn't it snow this week?"

"Oh sure," she says. She affects nonchalance by propping her feet up on his dashboard. "But I'm from Germany, you know? A little cold weather isn't going to stop us. If it did, we'd never get out of the house."

"You enjoying the States?"

She has been. She's been in California for three weeks. She tells Harrison that she graduated from a university in Heidelberg last month, and she decided to take at least the summer off. Maybe a year. "You don't mind if I take these off, do you?"

Harrison tells her he doesn't in a moment of automatic hospitality before he knows what she's going to take off. He's relieved when it's just her boots. "I've had these on for so long they're starting to become a part of me." She props her legs back up on the dash. "Now that I'm in America, I've been shaving every day." She waves a hand in front of her leg.

Harrison figures that he's supposed to go careening off the road at her boldness, but he just looks at the legs and nods. Since the divorce, he's noticed a sharp decline in his sex drive accompanied by an increase in women who are coming on to him. Not generally young women like Kirsten, but women his own age whose options are limited to the recently divorced and widowed. Most of these are old friends, and Harrison likes the attention, he has to admit to himself, but Kirsten reminds him of that kid in Sears, reminds him of his own son in an odd way. He just raises his eyebrow and says, "hmm."

*   *   *

The German boy in Sears looked hungry to Harrison all those years ago, but he couldn't exactly feed a child he wasn't related to. Carol noticed it too. This was back when they were still married. She'd come up behind him from women's clothing and found him talking to the little boy in his broken-down German. "We should take him to one of the employees."

Harrison hadn't said anything, didn't need to. He just stared at her meaningfully for half a second, and she'd nodded her agreement. The smells of hot dogs and grease were wafting in from the food court, and the boy turned in that direction trying to peer around people to see what the smell was. That could have been what he was doing, but Harrison might have been projecting on the kid.

They called out from where they were, asking if anyone were missing a child. No one stirred. Only a few even looked up from what they were doing. In the end, they decided to go down to the photo studio on the first floor. Halfway down the escalator, Harrison felt the little boy bounce. He pointed across the store to a family who were all in their Sunday best, all lined up outside the studio.

When they reached the first floor, he ran forward and next to what Harrison presumed was his sister, a dour-looking black-haired girl in a cornflower blue dress. She turned her head to inspect him when he reentered the family unit, but no one else did, not his two other brothers, his parents, or the old man Harrison assumed was his grandfather.

"Should we talk to them?" Carol had asked.

"And say what?"

*   *   *

Harrison finds himself telling Kirsten the story of the little German boy in the Sears department store because it seems to be just about the only thing the two of them have in common, and he's felt the need to talk more and more the longer she's sat there rubbing her smooth legs. "Yeah," she said. "In Germany, we don't have the paranoia that you have in the States over your children."

Harrison starts to respond, starts to say that there's a difference between not having paranoia and not knowing whether or not your own child is confused and lost in a country where he doesn't even know the language, but before he can do any more than just sputter a little, she says, "Look," and she points.

They have just crested a little hill, and down below them is a mother bear with a cub walking across the road. It's a scene straight off a post-card, and thinking that, Harrison puts the truck into park, grabs his camera, and gets out as quietly as he can. As an afterthought, he reaches in and grabs the keys. He doesn't know whether the action offends Kirsten, but he doesn't much care either.

Outside of the car, he clicks away at the camera. Occasionally, his photos make it into forestry service newsletters and once even on a brochure. His boss told him that he should make Harrison a photographer full-time in a flattering moment where he was only half-joking. This moment, Harrison knows, is full of potential. The bears wander off the road fifty yards ahead of him, and across a little weedy meadow. The grass is still low and there's still a patch or two of icy snow on the ground, and out in the middle of the meadow, the cub comes to a little log that the mother ambles over easily. It's too big for the cub though who stands on its hind legs with its forepaws on the log just as the mother turns around to watch her youngster. It's a moment filled with potential, and Harrison is clicking away composing it on the fly, lost in this perfect moment when

99

nature and art collide.

That's the moment when the screaming begins. Harrison has a second when his muscles contract into immobility, but when he realizes that it is Stanley, his son, screaming, Harrison launches himself in the direction of his truck, bears forgotten, photography career forgotten.

In the truck, Stanley is pressed back against his seat, staring at Kirsten and screaming. "Stanley," Harrison shouts. "Stan!"

He folds down the seat and grabs Stan by the wrists. He's found over the years that for some reason, this comforts the boy when he has episodes. The episodes are becoming more frequent as he gets older, and what the psychologists are doing seems to be making it all worse instead of better. Who knows though? Without them, it might have been terrible by now.

"Stan, Stan!" he yells until the boy has stopped screaming. "It's okay, Stan. She's not going to hurt you." He says that again and again until the boy calms himself, and Harrison's petting his head.

When the boy's finally calm and cried himself out, he looks at the girl. "Hi," she says merrily, as if nothing has happened. She offers her hand for Stan to shake. "I'm Kirsten. Are you Stanley?"

Stanley watches her for a worrisome moment when he might have any reaction, but finally, he giggles. "Hi Kirsten," he says, and he shakes her hand.

*   *   *

Harrison and Carol had watched the little German family in Sears for a long while as they chatted with an employee who almost certainly had to be the photographer. Harrison doesn't suppose he'd act the same way now, but he didn't have children then, and he was fascinated to watch the family dynamic, wondering how he might handle what was happening differently.

The parents were in a deep discussion with the man whom they must have found charming. He kept saying things that made them break into loud laughter, and the wife kept fake-slapping him on his chest and blushing. The kids in the meantime entertained themselves by investigating the world around them. This time, the little boy wasn't alone. He and his sister walked close to Harrison and Carol and into the washing machine section. The little girl found a front-loading dryer and opened it. She said something to the little boy who climbed in. Once he was in, his sister closed the door and wandered away.

It was too much for Carol, who came up behind the couple saying, "Excuse me. Excuse me!"

The couple turned toward Carol who told them what had happened to the boy. The woman laughed and shook her head. "Oh, he's always doing something like that," she said. She opened the door, and he crawled out. "Thank you for letting us know."

Carol was too stunned to tell the woman off, but all the way home, she'd given Harrison the speech that she should have said to the woman. By the time they were home, she was nearly in tears of anger and pity for the poor kids of "that horrible woman."

For some reason, and Harrison isn't sure what that reason was, he took the incident as proof that she was going to make a wonderful wife. He wishes now that he could go back and talk himself out of the naivete of that reaction.

*   *   *

After the initial shock has worn off, Stanley gets to like Kirsten. He asks her how old she is, and she says, "Five years old."

He narrows his eyes and looks at her doubtfully. "No you aren't," he says. But his voice says that he's not sure.

"No," she says. "You're right. I am ninety-five."

It takes a moment, but he realizes that she's joking, and he starts to giggle with her about it. "How old are you?" she asks.

"164," he says.

"Goodness. How old is your papa then?"

He starts laughing and cannot stop from laughing for a long while. When he starts to slow down, she makes a fart noise, and he starts laughing all over again. "Hey," she says finally, "do you want to see my tattoo?"

"What?" Harrison asks.

"Sure," Stanley says.

"My tattoo. I just got it a month ago, when I graduated." Before Harrison can say anything, she pulls the strap off her left shoulder and pulls down her tank top until the image of a dragon becomes clear on her shoulder blade.

"Cool," Stanley says. Again, Harrison feels that he should say something, but before he can, Stanley reaches out and strokes it with his finger.

"It's Fafner," she says. "Do you know Fafner?" Stanley doesn't respond, so she asks Harrison, "Do kids know Fafner in the States?"

"No," he says.

"Fafner was this dragon who had a big treasure that he got from killing many people. So the hero called Siegfried from the Netherlands searched him out." She gives Stanley a fairly detailed summary of the Nibelungenlied complete with sound effects of the dragon.

Stanley listens in rapt amazement, and she is able to focus in on what always captures his imagination. She talks about the ability of a single man to do great works, and the more she talks, the more he leans forward. By the time the man is bathing in dragon blood, Stanley's mouth is actually open, and he's focused in on her in a way that frightens Harrison a little. When Stanley is this focused, Harrison never knows where the boy's imagination is going to go. "He is like you, Stanley. He's a brave little soldier. He does good, you know?"

With the last words, Stanley takes a deep breath, and Harrison knows that this is the critical moment. The boy has made some kind of deep personal connection with something, but there's no way to know with what or in what way. Finally, he exhales and begins to weep.

*   *   *

Eventually, lecturing Harrison on the failings of parents she knew and saw became a sort of hobby for Carol. The image of that boy climbing into the dryer never really left her, and Harrison wondered if maybe talking about it afterwards had given her a kind of high, the kind that people get in church when condemning people from other churches to hell. She certainly seemed happy enough doing it.

Then she'd started to ask Harrison about his parents and their child rearing strategies. She'd ask about the big things at first. She wanted to know about education, sports, and religion, and she'd go over each part, telling him whether they'd succeeded or failed and to what degree that they'd failed. When she found out that he'd been spanked, she had nothing to say except to raise her eyebrows and snort. Eventually, she got down to the minutia that Harrison couldn't remember clearly, and when he didn't know how many chores he'd have to do over Christmas vacation or whether or not watching hockey was strictly forbidden because he never liked watching hockey to begin with, she'd become frustrated, and they'd get into a fight.

Why she was doing this was beyond him. They'd never discussed children, but suddenly she was kid crazy. That he never asked her why she'd become obsessed with other people's child-rearing techniques probably should have been a sign to him that they weren't going to make it as a couple, but it wasn't. He just kept on going frustrated and confused.

After they had Stanley, Harrison decided that she hadn't been planning it all that time. She was just thinking about child rearing because she was thinking about it. There was no ulterior motive. She was just at the right age and maybe there was something biological moving her, and when Stanley came along, he was overjoyed as much as she was, but there was still that difference. Whatever it was that stood between them and kept him from asking her basic questions was still there, and he came to realize that was what had killed the relationship.

*   *   *

"You're a sensitive little man, aren't you?" she asks Stanley. When Stanley doesn't respond, she turns to Harrison. "'Sensitive?' That's the word, isn't it?"

It certainly is a word, but he's not sure that's exactly what's going on with Stanley. Still, he says, "Sure."

"Ya, sensitive, but don't worry. It's a good thing. I've been all over California in the last few weeks, and I think your countrymen need to be more like you. Yes, you."

In the time that Kirsten has been in California, she apparently has become an expert on all of the personality defects of everyone in the country. Harrison might point out that people from Fresno, California don't necessarily have exactly the same opinions and character flaws that people from Mobile, Alabama or Detroit, Michigan do, but he doesn't bother. It's like it was with his wife when she'd bait him into the arguments about child rearing. Her mind is made up, and it seems to him that she's more interested in picking a fight than talking, so when she tells him that Americans aren't sensitive, he nods, and when later she says that American

103

are too sentimental, he nods again without pointing out an apparent contradiction. He's sure in any case that she'd come up with some meandering kind of logic that would make the contradiction disappear in her mind.

"When I first started my vacation," she says in the middle of a monologue about the lack of education in America, "all I did was find men in Bakersfield to have sex with."

Harrison glances into the rearview to see how Stanley's reacting to that one, but the boy doesn't seem to have noticed. He's staring out the window with half-closed eyes about to be lulled asleep by the road. Harrison wants to tell her to shut up about her sex life, but realizes that's what she wants him to do. She's looking for a way to criticize American's sexual mores, and he understands that the anger coming up in him is the anger that he used to feel for Carol when she would bait him.

So he decides to avoid the bait. "Really, in Bakersfield. That seems like an odd choice, but I hope you enjoyed yourself."

"Oh, sure, I guess, but that's not the point."

"Yeah, well, what's the point?"

"Well, the first time I go into someone's house, I check out their books, you know? The guys I was sleeping with, they didn't have any books. They were just watching television, and a couple of them had stacks of pornography."

"Yeah, well, Bakersfield has a notoriously good public library system. They were probably just checking them out there."

"Oh, yeah?" She's serious, and seems a little confused. Maybe she's wondering if she needs to reevaluate the entire culture based on this new information that she's received. It must be, Harrison decides, quite an experience for her to have to question an assumption.

Whether she's thinking about that or something else, she falls silent. He's still glad, he decides, that he picked her up. Out here, she's vulnerable, more so because she's so sure of herself. It's part of being that age to have that kind of confidence. He certainly did when he was where she is now, and he's sure that he annoyed the people around him.

He's finding himself growing sympathetic toward her, smiling at his memory of himself when he was her age, and he kind of wishes he had that all back. He's in the middle of a romantic image of himself when she says, "Oh look."

He tromps on the brake, and he and his son turn to where she's pointing. "A raccoon," she says.

Photographs of raccoons are fairly easy to get, and besides, few people really get excited about them the way they do for mountain lions or bears, so Harrison just sits and watches the animal. It must be exciting to see a raccoon for a European, and Stanley's always excited about any creature that he can anthropomorphize.

"It's beautiful," she says. "Boy or girl?"

Harrison doesn't know enough about the creatures to be able to tell, but he says, "male," trying to keep from giving her any ammunition to criticize him with. He used to lie to Carol this way too. He wishes that he could go back now and tell his younger self to keep away from Carol, that the two of them just weren't built for each other any more than he was built to be with Kirsten.

"Ah," she says. "Why is he limping?"

The animal is plodding across the dirt road, and yes, it has a pronounced limp in its front leg. "It must be injured," Harrison says.

They all watch it limp slowly along, and now that it's in the sunlight, Harrison's glad he didn't bother to take its picture. People only really like pictures of pretty animals. This raccoon's on its way out, clearly. It has the limp and patchy fur, and it's far too skinny. He's not sure how long raccoons live, but he'd be surprised if this one made it to the weekend without being eaten by something.

"We have to help it," Kirsten says. "Someone has to save it."

In the back seat, Stanley is coming more and more to life. He's sitting up straighter and watching more closely. His eyes are beginning to shine with the possibility of his father becoming the Siegfried of the raccoon world.

"Jesus Christ," Harrison mutters.

* * *

As far as Harrison could tell, after the divorce, Carol's hobby morphed. Now, she wasn't criticizing the parenting skills of random people who moved in and out of her life. Now, she just focused completely on Harrison's failures with Stanley. That was natural enough, he supposed. And if he were fair, the divorce had brought out of him all the things he found disagreeable about her, but after a while, he found himself modifying his behavior because he knew that when Stanley came home she'd question him about what he'd seen Harrison do when they were alone. Harrison wasn't lying exactly, but he was sneaking around and hiding his behavior.

He stopped keeping magazines of any kind out while Stanley was around. The boy had been flipping through his *Harper's* one weekend, and Harrison came home to a message on Monday night telling him that she didn't really care if he used pornography or not, but he should keep his dirty magazines away from her son. When he called back and said that it had just been *Harper's*, she clearly didn't believe him.

He stopped keeping beer in the house and put it in the garage when his son was around after she told him that she was thinking about requesting sole custody until he had gotten the help that he needed. He yelled at someone in traffic in front of Stanley, and she told him afterwards that she didn't need her son coming home with that kind of language. When he thought about asking Stanley not to reveal every little detail to his mother, he realized that he didn't want to put his son in that position. It wasn't fair to the boy to have to lie to his mother.

Whatever her game was, she was clearly winning it and winning at the divorce too. She was still controlling his life. It came to a sort of head when she called and said, "I don't care what you do in your private life. Date whomever you want, but just don't parade your women in front of my son. It's a bad influence."

"I want to remind you," he said, "that the reason for our divorce was that you cheated on me, and that Joey's currently living at your house." That wasn't strictly true. The divorce had happened because they didn't love each other, and Joey had just been the last straw, but it felt good to say.

And it was clear enough that she didn't care so much about what Stanley saw, but she wanted to control what Harrison was doing. That was how it felt, so Harrison made a point of having women stop by for dinner when Stanley was over. He tried to get as many different women as he could. Most of them were just friends or colleagues, people he knew and liked but had no interest in dating, but he was going to win this thing, so he invited them over and thought about Carol as she heard the litany of women he was having fun with. It was pathetic, certainly, but pleasant, too.

*   *   *

106

"Don't be like that," Kirsten says. "Don't be so *typically* American." Harrison can't decide whether he wants Carol to think that he has slept with the young, tattooed German hitchhiker or not. It comes down to a question of how much he wants to hurt his ex-wife.

"Dad," Stanley says, "you have to save the raccoon. He's someone's son." Stanley invests all his young passion into the word "son." The word must mean something to him.

"Do you remember when we talked about the circle of life?" Harrison asks. They'd done that after watching *The Lion King* for the fortieth time.

"Ach," Kirsten says in disgust.

"Dad, you have to do something."

Now of course, this is going to be the moment that Stanley talks about most when he gets back to his mother, and it's no win. If Harrison doesn't help the animal, he'll get a rundown of how cruel he is, and if he does help the animal, she'll be angry with him for endangering her son. The only choice he has is to find a way to diffuse this moment, and possibly to make something else more interesting in Stanley's memory.

In any case, he realizes, he has to get out of the car. "Hold on a moment. I need to get my gear." He says it as though dealing with damaged raccoons is a regular part of his job, and in fact he has special raccoon gear in his truck for all such occasions. He does have a broom handle in the bed of his truck from a broom he drove over in his garage, so he grabs that and a bag, although what he's supposed to do with either of them is beyond him. What exactly does Kirsten expect of him? Is he going to take the animal home and raise it until it's strong enough for raccoon immortality?

In any case, the two of them see his stick and bag and seem to be mollified by them. Kirsten even smiles and says, "See. Your papa is going to save the little man."

Stanley bounces up and down in his seat.

"Stay here," Harrison says. He crouches low and walks on the balls of his feet as though he is sneaking up on the animal. He circles wide, giving it time to move into the brush and out of sight of the truck. Harrison himself crests a little hill and then sits down on the other side with his back against a tree trunk. He watches the raccoon limp slowly away and wonders exactly what is going to eat it. Do raccoons cannibalize the weak? Harrison doesn't know, but he ponders this question and others as he waits an appropriate length of time.

Finally, he wanders back to the truck, smiling broadly.

"What happened?" Kirsten asks. "You didn't get him."

Harrison climbs into the truck, turns it on, and starts driving. "Didn't have to. He's an old one, and raccoons take care of their old. After a while, he limped back to his family who took him in and cared for him. No, the cruelest thing I could have done was take him away from a family like that, so I let him go."

Kirsten nods doubtfully, but Stanley is smiling and bouncing in the back, sure that his father did the right thing. How will Carol spin this now? He's sure that she'll find some way to make this the worst possible choice that he could have made. She'll say that Stanley could have gotten rabies or that he should never be lied to. The only way he can possibly avoid this particular lecture is to get her to focus on something else.

Harrison's thinking about this when he turns onto the main highway and towards a crossroads. "Where are you thinking about going?" he asks. "Where can I drop you?"

"Well," she says as she puts her boots back on. "I was thinking about going to Fresno tonight. You can leave me at the junction up there. Or I could," she pauses for a moment, "stay with you two tonight."

And this, of course, is the perfect distraction from the raccoon. When Stanley describes the hitchhiker who stayed with them for a few nights, Carol will hear about how young she was, and how nice she was, and how pretty she was. Carol will hear about the tattoo, and how she was so much fun to be around. The image of Harrison replacing her with someone twenty years younger than she is will burn Carol from the inside. She'll obsess about that in a way that she never obsessed about child rearing. She will feel what he felt when he found out about Joey.

He thinks about this as he tells Kirsten that he'll drop her at the junction. He tells her that he hopes she enjoys the rest of her trip and that the libraries in Fresno are even more famous than those in Bakersfield. He wonders how he's going to eclipse the raccoon in the boy's memory if he doesn't have his hitchhiker around, and he supposes that maybe he won't.

It doesn't matter too much, of course. If it weren't a lecture on the dangers of rabies from strange raccoons, he'd get a lecture on something else. It's something like love, he decides that keeps Carol lecturing. It's not love exactly, but it is possibly the closest thing to love that she can feel for him. And maybe he made a mistake not spending a few wonderful days with Kirsten. He watches her out of the rearview and thinks that maybe he has, as she shoulders her bag and begins to trudge down the hill with her thumb out to traffic. He's sure that she'll be safe though, and happier with the boys down in Fresno than she ever could have been with him.

Bear as Metaphor

Harrison's truck bounces to a stop on the rutted dirt road to his father's house when the bear, skinny and rangy by ursine standards, but giant by any other standard, shambles across the road thirty feet ahead of him. It's turning towards summer now, but up here in the Sierras, the snow still lies in patches in the places where the canopy of pines creates permanent shade. The animal is no doubt young, but he's also been hibernating long enough that he's gone thin, gaunt even.

By bear standards at least.

Of course, by Harrison's standards, the animal is huge. He's been driving now for hours with no radio, just the humming sounds of his truck tires on asphalt, and the meditation that comes with that droning sound makes his thoughts take a left turn. What he thinks about when he sees the bear is how much the animal reminds him of his father.

He doesn't think about it in those terms, but he just kind of sees the bear and his father for one moment as the same creature. In his mind, there is no difference between the two of them. The bear moves on across the road, and Harrison shakes out his mind and puts the car back in gear.

There are any number of reasons his mind went this direction, he thinks as he drives on. The first and most obvious is that he's on his way to his father's house. The old man lives at the end of the dirt road, cut off from anyone, and as far as he knows, Harrison will be the first person the old man will have seen for long months and months. The old man has been by himself in the snow, hibernating like that bear all winter.

It's an obvious metaphor, and one that Harrison shakes his head at, but that's probably the second thing that made his strange idea.

But really, Harrison realizes, the bear reminds him of the old man because there was a time when he looked like that bear. No, that's not exactly it. It's just that to Harrison's childhood eyes, his father was like that bear – wiry and rangy for a man, but powerful beyond the scope of a child's

110

imagination. His father had been infinitely strong and infinitely wise, and he seemed to shamble and stalk around. Harrison had been mesmerized by the old man, and a little afraid to approach him for fear of raising his ire and being swiped. He'd once had the same reverence and fear for his father that some people reserved for their gods, and he supposes, that he has a bit of that emotion still.

That's it, Harrison decides. That's what he was feeling when he saw the bear.

It's been an open debate this whole winter whether Harrison would find the man alive or dead when he came back up in the summer. Some had said yes, but Harrison had said no, unequivocally no. Everyone agreed that it wouldn't be tragic for him to die out here alone. It would have been exactly what the old man would have wanted, and the repeated mantra had been that it's not tragic to die doing what you love. It's only tragic not to.

But Harrison has never said that about his father. The fact is that he can't imagine the old man dying. Not this winter, not ever. To Harrison, he will always be eternal, an old bear wandering around his timeless forest. It's not healthy to think of his father in this way. Harrison knows that, but he can't shake the feeling either. He will always be the little boy to the great man. These are the kinds of thoughts Harrison's having when he climbs out of his truck in front of his father's house. It's an old cabin, the end of this dirt road that used to be a logging road for a group of Mormons long gone. Now the cabin's the only thing on it. If he thinks of it logically, his father should have died up here this winter. He's old now, pushing eighty, and to live up here by himself through the winter with no heat but a fire and no phone or Internet or way of contacting help if he should be hurt or confused – well, the old man should be dead.

"Dad," Harrison calls from his truck. He waits a beat. Generally, his father would have come out of the house by now, as soon as he heard Harrison's truck bumping its way over the ruts of the road. "Dad!" Harrison yells again.

But his dad doesn't respond. Maybe the old guy really did die in there, but that kind of thought isn't real to him. Instead of running to the front door, Harrison ambles across the yard, past the wood pile and bee hive the old man keeps.

The thing is that it wouldn't have to be a slip and fall. The man keeps bees in a cage in a part of the world where bear are thick. Normally, a California bear wouldn't attack a man, but his father keeps honey caged so the bear can't get it. Add ursine hunger and frustration and maybe the bear would. But when Harrison comes through the front door into the tidy cabin, it's clear that no one's died inside and there's no sign of blood. If the man is dead, he's dead somewhere outside the cabin. "Dad," Harrison calls. There's no movement upstairs or down just a silence in the clean room. It's been a long drive up here, so Harrison stretches out on the couch and is soon off to sleep.

The late afternoon sunlight is slanting in when Harrison wakes up. He blinks twice, stands up and calls once again for his father. He has the same feeling now that he did when he was a child and woke up from a nightmare. Then he called for his father, and his father came to him. No such luck now. He checks his watch, but he's not exactly sure what time it was when he fell asleep so there's no point.

Out in front of the house, the air is beginning to chill a little.

This is the way it's going to happen, Harrison realizes. At least, he hopes that this is how it will happen. The old man will simply disappear one day. No one will know where or how he met his death. No one will even be sure that he actually has died. He will simply not be there any longer. Everyone is right. Dying this way is the best. It's much better than sitting around a hospital for years wasting and dreaming of the man he used to be.

So Harrison sits on the front porch and dreams his gloomy thoughts. The light is beginning to slant away, and his father should be coming back home now, no matter where he went. He's probably just poking around the forest now that there's some warmth after the long winter, but he'll come back before dark. If the old man is alive, he'll be back before darkness closes in.

The sunlight lights up the trunks of the trees now. Harrison decides to play a game with the light. If his father is not back before the sunlight is lighting up only the treetops, Harrison will know that his father has died.

What will he do then? Harrison supposes that he'll drive down the mountain until he has a cell signal and call it in. They'll send out dogs maybe. Maybe they'll send a crew, but it won't matter. They'll just be looking for the man's body, and Harrison will hope that they won't find him. He'll hope that his father can stay out in the forest, where he loved to live. It's what the old man would want, and it's what Harrison wants too.

He'll never stop being that kid who calls out for his father in the dark. It would be nice if from now until Harrison is old too that there is a chance that his father will call back to him. Harrison has always said that he's not a religious man, but maybe he's been wrong all these years. Maybe this is his religion. Maybe he worships in the Cult of the Bearman of the Sierra Nevada. It's not a large cult, but it's his. If he's lucky, his god has ascended now to that untouchable pine tree heaven, and Harrison will be free to worship him from below as any good disciple should.

Whether this happens today or in two years, Harrison realizes as he leans back to watch the sunlight in the trees, it's going to happen. The Bearman will die, and Harrison will stay here on earth dreaming of the day that he can join the old man's spirit in the sky.

The Sister

Harrison's just sitting down to dinner when there's a knock at his front door. He wouldn't normally answer it, but he can tell just from the sound that it's his son. It doesn't make sense that he'd be here, or that he'd knock, but by the time Harrison considers either of these things, he's across the apartment and opening the door to his boy and the stepfather.

Harrison goes down on his haunches to check Stanley, patting him down as though he might feel an injury that's not at first apparent. "It's all right," Joey says. "Nothing's wrong with Stan."

Harrison moves aside to let the two of them in. "Is it Carol then?"

"No, nothing like that," Joey says.

If it's not Stanley, and it's not his ex-wife, then none of this makes sense to Harrison. Why would Joey come here? Why would he bring Harrison's son? "I don't understand," Harrison says.

Joey sits on a chair and offers one to Harrison as though it's his place and not Harrison's. "It's not either of them," Joey says. Just by looking at Stanley and at the floor in front of him, Joey gets Stanley to sit down. He's in control now, as he is in the courtroom before a judge, or probably anywhere else he goes. "It's my sister," Joey says.

"Is she all right?"

"No," Joey says. "Not exactly. Not by a long shot. I've told you about her, haven't I?"

It's a question, but Joey and he both know that they've talked about the sister, who is a part of Joey's personal mythology, the bit he brings into show how charitable he is even in the face of inadequacy. She exists, in Joey's mind, to highlight his own benevolence. In Joey's stories, Stacy borrows money, uses drugs, has sex with strange men, and gets flat tires, and it is only because of her brother that she's able to make it through life. There is an element of truth to all of it, and maybe more than just an element, but Harrison wonders how he comes off in Joey's self-

114

aggrandizing stories.

"What's happened?"

"Well, she's been arrested for a DUI, and she needs someone to bail her out." He takes a breath. "She's been arrested in West Monte."

It's this second part that significant. It's not that she's been arrested and might have a drinking problem and definitely is in need of help but that she's been arrested in his town, where as the assistant district attorney, he might have to face some embarrassment.

"Listen, Harrison, I wouldn't normally ask you, but I thought about it, and you're the only person I can come to for something like this."

"Something like what?"

"I need you to bail her out." And it all becomes clear to Harrison now. Socially, Harrison's the only person Joey knows outside of the law community. He can't ask any of those people for help because that's the way gossip begins. Why he'd be afraid of such gossip doesn't make sense, but it's clearly something he lives in terror of.

Something else becomes clear as well. Joey could have called or come over by himself, but he brought Stanley. They boy's staring up at Harrison now clearly confused and worried, hoping that his father will take care of the chaos and pain that's just entered his life. Joey brought Stanley as emotional blackmail. "Look," Joey says, "don't worry about anything. I'll even pay for it all. All you'll have to do is pick her up." He says this last part begrudgingly as though by all rights Harrison should be footing the bill, but he's just benevolent enough to take care of it. Of course, his pose of generosity is a show for Stanley. He's making himself both victim and hero in the boy's eyes, and even if Harrison picks the sister up, he'll seem a little petty since Joey will even pay the bail.

It's at this moment that Harrison realizes that he hates the man. He didn't hate him before, not completely. It doesn't seem that way. Before all he'd done was break up Harrison's family by sleeping with his wife, but that didn't feel as manipulative as this.

The worst part, of course, is that Harrison finds himself ushering Stanley and Joey out of his apartment as he gets his coat and accepts an envelope thick with cash. Down on the street, Joey and Stanley wave to Harrison as he drives off. Joey has his hand on Stanley's shoulder, and Harrison wonders if this is meant for his or Stanley's benefit. If it is for Harrison, is it meant to be a threat, emotional blackmail, or thanks? He's not sure, but he knows that he'll devote a good deal of time to pondering the subject.

Hours later, sitting next to Stacy at a bar, Harrison decides that it was meant to be a threat. The threat wasn't clear at the time, but it was there. It was supposed to be in his mind when Harrison got down to the jail and realized that the envelope was filled with fives and tens and not nearly enough to bail out Stacy, who is on her fourth DUI. It was meant to be at the top of his mind when he called Joey over and over, and Joey didn't pick up his phone, and when he had to call a bail bondsman and had to put up his own collateral and when he signed the contract saying that he would be responsible for Stacy, whom he had never met before, about whom he'd only heard the worst possible things.

Now, he sits next to Stacy who's knocked back four shots to his one glass of beer so she can "calm her nerves." She's not a terrible person, Harrison decides. He wouldn't go out of his way to know her, but not surprisingly, she's not as bad as Joey's always said that she was. Once he got her out of jail, and she figured out who he was and why he was there, she chatted in a friendly way about football of all things. She said that they were missing the Sunday night game, and she never missed a game, which was eventually, how they found themselves here, in a bar watching the Steelers lose to the Giants in the pre-season.

In the past two hours, the two of them have become fast friends, bonding over football and mutual dislike for Joey, whom she describes as her adopted mother. Harrison might point out that Joey could have a fairly good reason to mother her, but he's too angry at what he perceives as a threat to say anything kind about the man. "Like you can't take care of yourself," he says.

She clinks glasses, downs her shot, and orders another. "Listen," he says, "it's none of my business, but . . ."

"I know," she says. She shakes her head in self-loathing. "I know. You don't have to tell me." The bartender puts a shot down in front of her. "I've got a problem, and this" she lifts up her glass, "is the worst thing I could do. You're right."

Harrison's seen this technique before. The alcoholic admits she's pathetic and keeps drinking anyway. He knows how it would play out. He could tell her and counsel her and argue with her, and she'd be completely impervious because it's impossible to argue with someone who's agreeing that she should change. That's all right though, because at this moment, the last thing he wants is to argue with her. "I'm sorry," Harrison says. "It's none of my business, and I shouldn't have butted in."

So when she orders another, he does too. Two is his limit, but by the time that the Giants have their moral victory -- moral because after all this is just the preseason -- he's feeling a little loose, and when she laughs at her own jokes, he laughs louder, and when she leans her head on his shoulder, he runs his fingers through her hair. When she eventually stands up to go to the bathroom and falls down on her ass, Harrison can see the bartender start to come over to kick her out, but Harrison lifts up a finger to the man who pauses, a little unsure of whether he should trust the lush's friend.

"Hey," Harrison says, "why don't we get out of here?"

"Well, all right," she says. She gets up and grabs him by the front of his shirt, pulling him close enough to kiss him on the cheek. It's not what Harrison meant, but he doesn't try to disabuse her of the idea. "Come on," she says, and she does her exaggerated drunk walk toward the front door. The bartender nods solemnly at Harrison.

Out in the parking lot, Stacy pushes Harrison up against his truck and kisses him on the neck, the kiss turning into a lick. Harrison supposes that he'd be disgusted with this normally, but he can't smell her whiskey breath over his own beer breath. "Are we going to your place?" she asks.

"Do you think this is a good idea?" Harrison asks her back.

She pushes him away for a moment. "You don't like what you see?"

"No, you're . . . great." And objectively, even through the boozy haze, he can see that she is. In her early forties, she's fit with long brown hair, and there is something about her that, while tragic, is undeniably good and kind. Goodness, and he doesn't think this is only the alcohol coursing through his veins, seems to emanate from her.

"You're worried that you'll be taking advantage," she says.

Harrison nods, an apology in his eyes.

"You'll be taking advantage of me, but I'll be doing the same thing back. I'm going to tell my brother all about this. You know what he'll say when I tell him that I slept with *you*?" Her "you" makes it sound like Harrison is the lowest of the low, convicted criminal, evil flaking off him and infecting those around him.

"You're going to tell your brother?"

"Sure."

"Well, then, it's my place I guess." Maybe then, Harrison reflects while driving to his apartment, he is evil. There is good that seems to shine out of Stacy, so maybe evil shines out of him. He's going to be too drunk to care tonight, however. Tonight will be all about pleasure. He's going to take pleasure in this woman, in her body and her touch, but he's also going to take pleasure in the thought of her brother, and what his face is going to do when he hears exactly what the threat that he made brought about.

Used Cars

Harrison brings his new used BMW up above eighty miles an hour only to blush when he hits eighty-five and allow himself to drift back down to seventy. He's in love, he decides, with the car. He loves that even though it's used, the car dealership took the time to spray it with nu-car smell. He loves the way the tires sound on the road, and he has to admit to himself that he loves that it was expensive.

Even used, the BMW is the most expensive thing that he's ever owned with the exception of the house, which he lost in the divorce, and buying it wouldn't have been possible except for two tragic windfalls that happened in the same month. First, Carol, the ex-wife, married another man, the man she said she had always truly and secretly loved, and his favorite uncle had died, leaving him an inheritance that would have taken him a couple of years to earn on his own.

The lawyer told Harrison that it was lucky Uncle Jim had waited to die until after Carol's wedding. "She couldn't have gotten it, could she?"

"Maybe yes, maybe no," the lawyer had said. "I got a feeler from her lawyer last week asking about it. I think that she wanted to tie the money to your visitation rights with Stanley."

Harrison had started to say something, thought of something else to say and then had come up with a question all at once so when he'd responded to this news, it had come out as a sputter, but the lawyer held his palm up. "No," he said with a self-confident smirk. "I shut that down well enough."

Somehow the lawyer's assurance didn't do much for Harrison's emotional health, and when he'd been complaining about the ex-wife at work to his boss, Deena had said, "I swear to God, she's the pushiest bitch I've ever known. I mean if any woman in your life deserves that money, it's me."

She hadn't been joking. That the two of them had been sleeping

119

together on and off for over a year was an open secret in the office, but he supposed that this was her odd way of trying to make their relationship official.

So Harrison asked for a week off and got it. He'd gone down to the used car dealership and bought the nicest used car he could find, left his cell phone at home and started driving north, straight out of Los Angeles, over the Grapevine and down through the central valley where no one would be able to find him.

Now, some place north of Bakersfield, his last conversation with Carol keeps running through his head. This was after the lawyer'd shut her down presumably, but before Harrison had heard anything about it. They'd been talking about the private music lessons that Harrison was paying for and the special school that Stanley was going to, and how they were going to have to make the time to drive the boy to his lessons. "Yeah, well, I guess that's not something you have to worry about too much," she'd said and laughed.

He hadn't thought about the comment before now. It had been strange, but pretty much all of the conversations they'd had since the divorce had been strange. They'd been amicable enough, but all of their lost love and anger and hurt had infected what they'd said to each other.

Could it be though, that this hadn't been just a stray remark that had come from the awkwardness of divorce? The more he thinks about it, the more it sounds as though she was telling him that she was going to try to block his custodial rights. He doesn't know if she could do that especially over his inheritance, but that doesn't mean that she isn't going to try. He finds himself thinking about his cell phone that's sitting on the dining room table in his apartment as he's coming into Delano, and he pulls off to look for a pay phone. There was a time when every gas station would have two or three pay phones sitting outside, but it takes three gas stations before Harrison finds a phone, and that one's missing the receiver. He finally finds a fast food place that has one, but as he stands there with quarters in his hands, he realizes that he's not sure what to say to her. He should probably just ask her the question, but he can't think of a way to put it.

In a moment, he's back on the road. It's ridiculous anyway. Carol might have her faults, but she's never tried to do anything to harm Harrison's relationship with Stanley. Whether she likes Harrison or not, she's always seen the bond between father and son as sacred and important to Stanley's development. No, that couldn't have been what she meant.

Harrison calms down and gets back into the rhythm of the drive pretty quickly. He lets himself fall into the trance that his new car can bring him into. It's strange. He's never really derived joy from an object before, and certainly toys have never moved him, but it's fun to cut through traffic smoothly finally not bouncing around in his old truck. His lack of interest in objects is one of those things that precipitated the divorce, he's pretty sure. It's not as though Carol ever gave him an ultimatum about the money that he made or even voiced her disapproval, but he'd known that she was disappointed with not taking vacations, not having nice things, that they'd lived in the tiny house he'd bought before they'd met.

Ironically, she'd gotten the house that she'd never liked in the divorce. And thinking about it, she'd gotten every single little thing that she'd wanted in the divorce, and when he'd start to complain, she'd say, "Listen, don't you want your son living in a house?" Or "Do you want your son to have to scrimp?" Whenever he complained, she had invoked their son, and it had worked every time until his Uncle Jim had died. The inheritance was the first time she'd been told no. And if using their son had worked before, wouldn't it make sense that she'd use Stanley this time too?

Harrison has this epiphany twenty miles south of Fresno, and it eats at him until he can pull off and find a pay phone. This time he plunks in his quarters and dials, but he doesn't seem to have enough quarters, and he has to go into the liquor store it's in front of to wait in a long line and get change. By the time he gets back, he's had enough time to brood over what he's going to say to Carol and to think of all the worst possible outcomes. He's had three variations of the argument in his mind, and now, he's obsessing over the version where she actually does try to get his custodial rights removed. In his mind, they're locked in a court battle for years, they both go bankrupt, despite his new money, and Stanley grows into a disillusioned and angry teenaged punk.

Harrison's nearly shaking with anger as he stands in front of the pay phone, and it is only with the calming repeated mantra, "She didn't do that. She didn't do that" that he can bring himself to pick up the phone and call. When her voice mail picks up, he realizes that it's still too early. She doesn't answer her cell during work unless it's a call from someone she knows like Stanley or Stanley's school. She generally would have taken Harrison's call, but her caller ID would have shown that either it was a pay phone or just an unknown caller.

In any case, Harrison can't think of anything to say on the message. He can't very well ask her to call back unless he's willing to sit here in this parking lot watching locals parade out bags of potato chips and cases of beer for the next couple of hours. Instead, he listens to her voice asking him to leave a message, and then he listens to the staticky sound of himself not leaving a recording. He's lost his quarters, so he cradles the phone, and looks at his watch. No, he'll just call back. Anyway, he's not going to ruin his vacation, his short bit of freedom, worrying about the ex-wife. He lost enough vacation days that way when he was married to her.

With Frenso behind him, he realizes though that it's obvious enough that she has already ruined this vacation. It's gone, and it's going to stay gone until he gets through to her so he can stop obsessing about this. So he speeds through Merced and doesn't stop. It's too soon to call her. She'll be working for a while now, and she probably won't be out of work when he's in Modesto either.

Deena was, of course, right. She is pushy and grabby, and even though he is still more than just a little in love with Carol, he's damn glad that they're divorced. He tries to imagine what it would be like married to her right now with this new bit of money. There would be no BMW, that's for sure. Not for him, anyway. On the other hand, Deena calling Carol pushy and then claiming the money as her own had been about as hypocritical as it could get.

Harrison tries to think back on his relationship with Deena, which has been almost entirely sexual, to find something that might have suggested that kind of closeness. They've had a couple of trips together, Stanley seems to like her well enough, and they've been happy a lot of the time, but there's been no talk of long term plans. In fact, until she called Carol a pushy bitch and made a claim on his finances, they'd both agreed that they were going to keep the relationship light and secret. There was, they had said, no good reason to start people in the office talking about something that might be completely casual, and unless and until they made some kind of commitment to each other, they were going to keep it to themselves. That was all true enough until Deena seemed to take control of the relationship in an incredibly public way.

It had been the same thing with Carol. They had been dating casually and just having fun until one day Harrison realized that she was calling her his fiance. When he'd asked her about it, she'd said, "Well, I mean come on. That's where we're headed isn't it?"

At the time, he'd found that endearing. Now, he can't remember how in the world he'd allowed it, let alone found a way to romanticize it. There was something about him that was passive and in fact wanted to be manipulated. God, he wishes that he could go back to that time and talk to himself. It's not that he wouldn't marry her. Maybe he would, but it would have been better if the relationship hadn't been about her making decisions that he found out about later.

Harrison pulls into Modesto and finds a pay phone. He doesn't stop there though. He drives around until he finds a bank and exchanges a twenty for two rolls of quarters. He goes back to the phone, dials, and talks, plunking in quarter after quarter for as long as he needs to. He hangs up fifteen minutes later, and when he does, he and Deena are broken up.

There's no chance that he's going to enjoy this vacation now, he decides, not until he has a conversation with Carol and probably not for hours afterwards. He'll need time to obsess over that conversation too. Maybe by tomorrow, if everything goes perfectly, he'll be able to relax. In any case, he points the BMW in the direction of a Best Western. He'll get a room and call from there. He'll be able to leave a message and wait by the phone in relative comfort. Maybe he'll call Deena too, but probably not. If he gets the urge, he'll have the conversation with himself that he wishes he could have had all those years ago.

Let Us All Pray Now to Our Own Strange Gods

Harrison wakes up to the warmth of his son's palm cradling his cheek. The boy is staring into his eyes maybe twelve inches from his face, and Harrison doesn't know how long Stanley's been there, but it feels like a long time. Stanley's expression is serious and brooding the way it gets when he's lost inside himself, and Harrison stares back for a moment, neither of them blinking, neither of them saying a word.

The fact is that Stanley's getting too old for this kind of thing. When he was three or four years old, it was cute, but the boy's rushing toward his teenage years, and those things that once made him an idiosyncratic scamp are turning into the things that make him a weird kid.

Still, Harrison doesn't say anything about it as the two get up and pack up the tents and sleeping bags. He doesn't want to break the magic of the father-son camping trip to the desert. Stanley's had good days lately, the kind of days he never seems to have since the divorce. Either the therapy is working, or he's growing out of a particularly awkward phase. In any case, he's had good days since this trip began.

They're going to see a ghost town today, "A real live ghost town," Harrison says to his son in the back seat of the truck. There aren't many of them around any longer and those that still exist have mostly been turned into Disneyesque profit making machines complete with gift shops and restaurants. The one they're headed for is an old abandoned mining town, too far back into the desert and too far up the mountain on a dirt road for anyone to have damaged it since it was abandoned over a hundred years ago. Harrison's been there before. As a part of the forestry service, he's gotten back to a lot of places few others have seen, so he knows it's not picturesque the way that those tourist traps are, but it's real, something the boy will remember even if he remembers nothing else from this trip.

"You'll have that limp for the rest of your life," Stanley says. He's speaking to one of his stuffed monkey. A little while ago, Harrison came

124

home to find it crucified in the garage and the rest of his puppets and stuffed animals sitting in a semi-circle of judgment staring at the martyr. Occasionally since then, Stanley will bring up the crucifixion in his long conversations with his monkey.

But Harrison doesn't really want to sit through another one of these conversations, so he says, "Hey Stan, what do you think about a ghost town. A real live ghost town."

"Are there ghosts?"

Harrison laughs. "I don't know. Maybe."

Stanley pauses for a moment considering. "How do you think that they died?"

He probably should have expected this kind of thing. Stanley wouldn't have had to have been a weird kid to come up with a question like that, but something in the boy's tone when he asks it makes Harrison swallow a little. "Nice deaths, I think." But he knows almost immediately what the follow up question to that it is going to be, "like the man who died from . . ." His voice peters out at the lameness of it all.

"Dad!" Stanley's voice is a warning, and Harrison realizes that he's taken his eyes off the road. Ahead of him, coming towards them, is the first truck they've seen all day, flashing its lights on and off.

Harrison pulls over to the side and rolls down his window, and the driver, a white-haired man, maybe sixty years old but with the shoulders of a gold miner, pulls up so they can talk. "Are you the ranger?" the old man asks.

Harrison's in his forestry service truck. He probably shouldn't have taken it on vacation, but he wanted something that could go up these old roads. "No," Harrison says. "Not officially, but do you need help?"

The man nods. "I think so. I found a dead body. A woman."

"Up in the mountains?" Harrison asks. He's trying to see if the man looks like a murderer or not. He has no idea what a murderer might look like, but there would be tell-tale signs, wouldn't there? There would be a shiftiness or a smoothness and a too-kind demeanor, a kind of charm, wouldn't there?

"Yeah," he says. "Just off the road, up there in an abandoned building."

"In the ghost town?" Stanley asks.

"Yeah," the man says.

"How do you think she died?"

The man stares at the boy for a moment, his eyebrows narrowing just a little. "I don't think it was bad," he says. "I think she was at peace."

Had Harrison been in any other vehicle, had he not offered the man help, he probably would have simply driven on, giving the man the advice to go down to the closest ranger station, which is nearly a hundred miles away, and report it. Somehow though, he feels responsible, and besides, there's Stanley in the back seat expecting his father to be the hero he thinks he is. So the man is in the cab now, riding in the passenger seat giving advice on how to get to a place that Harrison's seen twice before. When Harrison introduces himself and Stanley, the man says, "I'm Father Crandell."

"A Catholic priest?" Harrison asks.

"Yes," he says. Harrison doesn't know what to say. He wasn't expecting a priest, but he really hadn't been expecting anything. Still, the man doesn't fit Harrison's conception of a priest. He's too big. He's too vital. It's a prejudice based on nothing, Harrison knows, but his idea of a priest is an ascetic little man with a wheezing cough, not this vital old-timer touring the desert on his own.

"You're *really* a priest?" Stanley asks.

"Yes," Father Crandell says.

"Then tell me what a stigmata is."

"Stanley," Harrison says. There's a warning in his voice that his son shouldn't be rude, but the priest waves it away.

"It's the wounds of Christ," he says. "It's where he was crucified through his hands and his feet, and his other wounds, too." The priest adjusts in his seat to settle himself as Harrison crests a little hill. "Some of his saints have been blessed with the stigmata as a sign that they're doing God's work on earth."

"Like St. Francis?"

Father Crandell turns around to get a better look at Stanley. "Yes," he says, "like St. Francis." The priest narrows his eyes at Harrison in confusion, and Harrison tries to tell the old man not to worry about Stanley, that this is just something he does, that he likes people very much but that his conversations tend to race to the most awkwardly intimate concepts available. Harrison tries to say all of this with his eyes, and he

126

thinks that the priest actually does get all of that because he nods, and Harrison finds himself instantly liking the man.

Stanley leans back in his seat, and in his rearview, Harrison can see him inspecting the wounds in his stuffed monkey's hands. He's gotten too old to play with stuffed toys too, but Harrison hasn't said anything. He won't say anything either because he knows that the ex-wife wants him to. She wants Harrison to take the animals away so that she can comfort the little boy, perhaps give him a new stuffed animal and tell him that it will remain a secret between mother and son. He knows the ex well enough to know that she's fantasized and planned all of this.

So Harrison's going to let Stanley stay in his puppet dream world as long as the boy feels comfortable there. He's thinking about this as he watches his son in snatches and talks to the priest about his trip. "One of my parishioners," he is saying, "told me about the ghost town up here. It's not much of a town though."

"It's not what you see in the movies, that's for sure."

"I wasn't expecting that, but I thought there'd be more buildings. I mean, I thought it would be more of a town."

"Oh well, there's only a couple of structures left, but did you see the foundations for the others? And there's the mine, too."

"No," he says.

"Well, the mine ran out and the people left and those who stayed in town for a while either used the boards to build things, or they burned them on cold nights. The remnants of the old houses are everywhere."

"I guess I missed that."

Harrison shrugs. "They're easy to miss. I mean they're all over the place, but if you don't know what you're looking at, you're not going to see them. I could give you a tour."

Out of the corner of his eye, Harrison can see the priest shake his head. "She's not going to get any deader from me showing you around."

"No," he says, and his voice is muted. Harrison would have thought that a priest would be used to death after having given last rites his whole career. Isn't death, after all, ultimately what priest are always talking about? Isn't that what they're getting everyone ready for? Shouldn't the man be comfortable with the idea? Whether he should be or not, it's clear that he simply isn't. "She's on the second floor."

Harrison nods. There's no need to elaborate. There's only one two

127

story building in the place. "How is she?"

It takes a moment for the priest to understand what Harrison is asking, and then it takes another moment for him to formulate his answer. "Fresh," he finally says. "I think she must have just died yesterday."

"How'd it happen?"

"I don't know. It wasn't violent, though, not as far as I could tell. I should have carried her out of there."

"No, you shouldn't have. You did the right thing." Harrison says. He tells the priest to shut up with his eyes for the sake of Stanley, and again, Father Crandell seems to understand the message. He nods his head, and the two of them descend into a sullen silence.

"St. Francis was able to talk to animals," Stanley says eventually from the back seat. Father Crandell turns to look at the boy, so Stanley says, "St. Francis could do a lot of things."

"That's true," Father Crandell says, and they all lapse back into the silence.

It can't be a lot of fun for Stanley, Harrison realizes, but on the other hand, the boy's going to remember it all. In the battle he and the ex have waged over the boy's affection, this is going to be one on Harrison's side. She has stability and the new wealthy husband to make Stanley's life better. Harrison has moments like these to fight back with. She can buy him what he wants, and Harrison can show him the oddities of the national parks.

Eventually they crest the ridge where the road widens out. Harrison turns left, and they arrive at what is left of the ghost town in another ten minutes. It is as Harrison remembers it, one building fallen down on itself completely and the other two leaning as though they are about to fall. They have been leaning that way for the last fifty years or so, but both times he's seen them, he's been sure that they're going to tip over before he leaves that day.

Harrison drives up to the front door of the two story building and sits there in park for a moment before going in. He's no more interested in seeing the woman than Father Crandell is, but he comforts himself with the knowledge that death isn't his business, not the way it is with a priest. It never has been.

He's had to pull out only one other body in his career with the forestry service. That time he was in the back country on foot and happened to run into a ranger. The poor guy had to transport a body from

128

deep under the trees to a clear spot where the helicopter was going to land. The man had asked for help without telling Harrison how bad it was going to be. When they got to the body, it had been dead for a while. The stench was unbearable, and something had eaten most of it. The dried blood and torn away face stayed with Harrison for months as did the bugs crawling through it. The worst was that the person, and Harrison never found out if it had been a man or a woman, had been lying against a log. When they pulled the body away there was the distinct sound of dried blood ripping away from the smooth trunk.

That's what Harrison expects, but when he steps out of the truck, he knows it's going to be better than that this time. If nothing else, there's no smell out here. The priest was right. She must have just recently died, maybe even a few hours ago because the smell comes out of a corpse quickly. He goes into the leaning house and onto the stairs, pausing a moment at the bottom stair, which seems sturdy enough. The people who owned this house, when they left, must have thought the wood on the ground floor was more valuable than all the rest of the wood because they ripped it out, leaving the rest of the place intact. It's not a friendly house. No paint inside, no wallpaper, just bare wooden walls, and Harrison imagines what a relief it must have been to finally have moved away from this place. Harrison stares at the odd old room for a moment, taking in the musty smells of the past until he has the strength to move on.

Up on the second floor, he sees her immediately. He doesn't want to touch her, not yet, not until he absolutely has to, so he goes down on his haunches five feet from her. Her face is turned away from him, but she has dark black hair. She's thin the way teenagers are, and Harrison guesses from here that that's what she is. She has little green shorts and a dark gray tank top on, and her skin is ashen. She has taken her boots off, and her feet are covered in painful-looking blisters.

Father Crandell's right. Whatever she died of, it wasn't violent. There's not a mark on her smooth skin. Nothing mars it, and she seems almost comfortable with a t-shirt for a pillow. There's a pink backpack propped in the corner of the room with a badge on it that says, "Girls Rule!" The backpack probably explains it. The young girl thought that she had more strength than she actually did and started to hike in the desert, making her way to the ghost town. It would have been impossible to carry the amount of water that she needed, so she probably just collapsed here and couldn't go any farther. She came upstairs because the floorboards were gone downstairs. It wasn't a bad plan. The house would have kept her out of the sun at least, but it doesn't seem to have saved her.

Poor kid. Poor weird kid. Harrison likes the weird kids the most, of course. These are the ones who live in their heads, dreaming. The problem with the dreamers is that when they hit eighteen, they decide to do things like hike through the desert by themselves. She probably came up to this ghost town with her parents ten years ago, and daydreamed about walking out here on her own. Weird kids come up with that kind of thing, and that's what makes them interesting, but it's also what makes them dead. The children of the herd are dull but safe. They stay in malls and flirt in the same way that their parents did and then they have conventional children who say and do the same things that their parents and grandparents did. Weird kids have weird dreams and go out to do weird things, and . . . but Harrison can't think about that any longer, somehow out of nowhere he's thinking about the stigmata on Stanley's stuffed animal, and he's crying. It's always the goddamn weird kids, he thinks one last time, and he forces himself to push those kinds of thoughts out of his head.

In a moment, he has control of himself, and he's wiped his face off and is climbing down the stairs. Outside, he's stopped by the sight of his son. The boy's crawled up into the passenger seat next to the priest. He has his hand on the old man's face, and he's staring into the old man's eyes. Father Crandell's expression can be described only as befuddlement. He looks as though he wants to tell the boy to stop, but he's too kind.

"Stanley!" Harrison yells. Whatever spell had held the boy and the priest there is broken now and the two of them blink at Harrison. Harrison wants to yell something more, but what is there to yell? How to yell at a boy to stop being weird and to become a part of the mass of herd animals that make up society so he doesn't end up dead in the second floor of an abandoned building when he's eighteen? So he just says, "Stanley," again.

The two of them, boy and priest, climb out of the truck. "I'm sorry," Harrison says to the priest.

Father Crandell waves it off and comes over to him. Stanley stretches and stares at the view wandering, thankfully, away from the priest and the building. "No, I'm sorry, sometimes he . . ."

"Don't worry about it," Father Crandell says. "We were just talking. He wanted to know more about St. Francis. I hope it's all right that I told him what I know."

How a conversation about St. Francis could lead Stanley to cup a priest's cheek with his hand is beyond Harrison, but it seems enough just to know that Stanley's a weird kid. It had been strange enough for Harrison who woke up to his son doing that to him, but he can't imagine how awkward it was for the priest who doesn't know the boy.

"What are you going to do about the girl's body?" Father Crandell asks.

"I was going to put her in a fireman's lift and carry her down here, but I couldn't bring myself to do it. I just couldn't throw her over my shoulder, you know?"

The priest nods. "You don't want help, do you?"

Clearly, the man wants Harrison to say no, but he can't imagine himself being that intimate with that girl. He can't see himself holding her close to his body and thinking about what has happened to her. Just standing in the same room with her brought him to tears. How could he hold her and tend for her and then make it down the mountain?

"I thought we could wrap her up in my sleeping bag and maybe make a litter out of something."

Father Crandell, Harrison decides, must make a pretty good priest. He doesn't want to be here, clearly doesn't want to be doing this, but he swallows and nods to Harrison. He's pale enough that Harrison thinks he might throw up, but Harrison figures that he looks about the same.

Probably, the priest was a weird kid, too. Harrison certainly was. Both let their imaginations and emotions run away with them in ways that are obviously not healthy. But the problem is that this here is the job of adults. It's the job of men, and moreover it's the job of people in the forestry service and of priests. They should be able to do this with grim resolve, but neither of them can seem to get beyond their own thoughts and imaginations. What they need is one of the herd people. Those people have cliches and examples to fall back on. They trust what their parents said, and they have only to act like their parents to make everything all right.

The two of them walk over to the only other building still standing in this old town. It's a house too, but crumbling a little more than the other. Harrison finds a spot where the boards have pulled away from the house a little over the years. He grabs one and wrenches it out of its nails revealing the room on the inside of the house. He grabs a neighbor board and pulls it free as well.

"It's not going to be a very good stretcher," Father Crandell says.

"No, but it just has to get her down the stairs. I just don't want to touch her any more than I have to." But of course, he realizes that they don't need a stretcher at all, not for any reason. When he puts her in the sleeping bag, they can just grab either side of that.

He puts his hand against the old building and says a silent prayer that it won't fall down any time soon even with this new insult to its structure -- it's a weird thought, he knows -- and while he's in the middle of that, Father Crandell says, "Where's Stanley?"

Harrison looks around, looks across the dirt road, looks down past the truck. He looks everywhere that the boy could be, but he already knows exactly where Stanley went. "Oh, God," he says.

The two of them jog to the two story house, but something makes Harrison take the stairs slowly. He doesn't want to scare the boy, he supposes, who must already be traumatized by the dead girl upstairs, and if Harrison thought that his son was strange before, he has the feeling that the boy is going to be completely unknowable now.

He expects Stanley to be in hysterics or comatose or he doesn't know what, but when he enters the room, he's surprised by his son once more. Stanley's crouched over the girl. His palm is cradling her face, exactly the way it was with Harrison that morning, exactly as it was with Father Crandell.

"Stanley," Harrison says, but Stanley doesn't move. He's staring down at that girl with that same serious intensity that he always gets at such moments. He's been there a while, Harrison thinks. Stanley's chewing on his bottom lip, which is bright red now. "Stanley," Harrison says again, this time louder, more commanding.

But Stanley still doesn't move. He's gone to his own world now, he's concentrating as only weird little boys can concentrate, and just as Harrison is about to come into the room and pull his son away from the girl, she takes a single deep breath. Now, it's Harrison's turn to be quiet and just to stare while she reanimates. First, her fingers twitch. Then her legs adjust themselves for comfort. Finally, she opens her eyes and blinks twice only to stare up at Stanley. They are locked together like that for a moment of silent communication that only they can know until finally she says, "Hello."

Stanley smiles, the first smile that Harrison's seen from the boy all

132

day long. "Hello," he says back.

It's a long way back down the mountain for the four of them. The girl, of course, needs help to the truck and the priest sits in the back with her, tending to her blistered feet as well as he can, but Stanley sits up in the passenger seat next to his father. In the back wheel well, his stuffed monkey lies silently unattended, but all the way down, Stanley inspects his own palms, back and front again and again waiting, Harrison assumes, for that first single drop of blood.

About the author

John Brantingham's work has appeared in hundreds of magazines in the United States and England, and his poetry has been featured on Garrison Keillor's *Writer's Almanac*. His other books include *Mann of War* and *East of Los Angeles*. He teaches at Mt. San Antonio College in Walnut, California where he lives with his wife, Ann.